Timbuktu

Paul Auster is the bestselling and critically acclaimed author of *The New York Trilogy*, *Moon Palace*, *The Music of Chance*, *Leviathan* and *Mr Vertigo*. He has published several volumes of essays, poems and translations, as well as the memoir *Hand to Mouth*. He has been described as 'a genius of a novelist' (*Sunday Telegraph*) and 'a master of the modern American fable' (*Telegraph*).

Timbuktu

PAUL AUSTER

ff

faber and faber

First published in 1999
by Faber and Faber Limited
3 Queen Square London WC1N 3AU
This open market edition first published in 1999

Photoset by Agnesi Text, Hadleigh
Printed in England by Mackays of Chatham plc, Chatham, Kent

© Paul Auster, 1999

Paul Auster is hereby identified as author of this
work in accordance with Section 77 of the Copyright,
Designs and Patents Act 1988

*This book is sold subject to the condition that it shall not, by
way of trade or otherwise, be lent, resold, hired out or otherwise
circulated without the publisher's prior consent in any form of
binding or cover other than that in which it is published and
without a similar condition including this condition being
imposed on the subsequent purchaser*

A CIP record for this book
is available from the British Library

ISBN 0-571-20104-0

2 4 6 8 10 9 7 5 3 1

for Robert McCrum

Timbuktu

Mr. Bones knew that Willy wasn't long for this world. The cough had been inside him for over six months, and by now there wasn't a chance in hell that he would ever get rid of it. Slowly and inexorably, without once taking a turn for the better, the thing had assumed a life of its own, advancing from a faint, phlegm-filled rattle in the lungs on February third to the wheezy sputum-jigs and gobby convulsions of high summer. All that was bad enough, but in the past two weeks a new tonality had crept into the bronchial music – something tight and flinty and percussive – and the attacks came so often now as to be almost constant. Every time one of them started, Mr. Bones half expected Willy's body to explode from the rockets of pressure bursting against his rib cage. He figured that blood would be the next step, and when that fatal moment finally occurred on Saturday afternoon, it was as if all the angels in heaven had opened their mouths and started to sing. Mr. Bones saw it happen with his own eyes, standing by the edge of the road between Washington and Baltimore as Willy hawked up a few miserable clots of red matter into his handkerchief, and right then and there he knew that every ounce of hope was gone. The smell of death had settled upon Willy G. Christmas, and as surely as the sun was a lamp in the clouds that went off and on every day, the end was drawing near.

What was a poor dog to do? Mr. Bones had been with Willy since his earliest days as a pup, and by now it was next to impossible for him to imagine a world that did not have his master in it. Every thought, every memory, every particle of the earth and air was saturated with Willy's presence. Habits die hard, and no doubt there's some truth to the adage about old dogs and new tricks, but it was more than just love or devotion that caused Mr. Bones to dread what was coming. It was pure ontological terror. Subtract Willy from the world, and the odds were that the world itself would cease to exist.

Such was the quandary Mr. Bones faced that August morning as he shuffled through the streets of Baltimore with his ailing master. A dog alone was no better than a dead dog, and once Willy breathed his last, he'd have nothing to look forward to but his own imminent demise. Willy had been cautioning him about this for many days now, and Mr. Bones knew the drill by heart: how to avoid the dogcatchers and constables, the

paddy wagons and unmarked cars, the hyp-
ocrites from the so-called humane societies. No
matter how sweetly they talked to you, the word
shelter meant trouble. It would begin with nets
and tranquilizer guns, devolve into a nightmare
of cages and fluorescent lights, and end with a
lethal injection or a dose of poison gas. If Mr.
Bones had belonged to some recognizable breed,
he might have stood a chance in the daily beauty
contests for prospective owners, but Willy's sidekick was a hodgepodge of genetic strains – part
collie, part Labrador, part spaniel, part canine
puzzle – and to make matters worse, there were
burrs protruding from his ragged coat, bad
smells emanating from his mouth, and a perpet-
ual bloodshot sadness lurking in his eyes. No one
was going to want to rescue him. As the homeless bard was fond of putting it, the outcome was
written in stone. Unless Mr. Bones found another
master in one quick hurry, he was a pooch
primed for oblivion.

   "And if the stun guns don't get you," Willy
continued, clinging to a lamppost that foggy
morning in Baltimore to prevent himself from
falling, "there's a thousand other things that will.
I'm warning you, kemo sabe. You get yourself
some new gig, or your days are numbered. Just
look around this dreary burg. There's a Chinese

restaurant on every block, and if you think mouths won't water when you come strolling by, then you don't know squat about Oriental cuisine. They prize the taste of dog, friend. The chefs round up strays and slaughter them in the alley right behind the kitchen – ten, twenty, thirty dogs a week. They might pass them off as ducks and pigs on the menu, but the in-crowd knows what's what, the gourmets aren't fooled for a second. Unless you want to wind up in a platter of moo goo gai pan, you'll think twice before you wag your tail in front of one of those Chink beaneries. Do you catch my drift, Mr. Bones? Know thine enemy – and then keep a wide berth."

Mr. Bones understood. He always understood what Willy said to him. This had been the case for as long as he could remember, and by now his grasp of Ingloosh was as good as any other immigrant who had spent seven years on American soil. It was his second language, of course, and quite different from the one his mother had taught him, but even though his pronunciation left something to be desired, he had thoroughly mastered the ins and outs of its syntax and grammar. None of this should be seen as strange or unusual for an animal of Mr. Bones's intelligence. Most dogs acquire a good working knowledge of two-legged speech, but in Mr. Bones's case there was the advantage of being blessed with a master who did not treat him as an inferior. They had been boon companions from the start, and when you added in the fact that Mr. Bones was not just Willy's best friend but his only friend, and then further considered that Willy was a man in love with the sound of his own voice, a genuine, dyed-in-the-wool logomaniac who scarcely stopped talking from the instant he opened his eyes in the morning until he passed out drunk at night, it made perfect sense that Mr. Bones should have felt so at home in the native lingo. When all was said and done, the only surprise was that he hadn't learned to talk better himself. It wasn't for lack of earnest effort, but biology was against him, and what with the configuration of muzzle, teeth, and tongue that fate had saddled him with, the best he could do was emit a series of yaps and yawns and yowls, a mooning, muddled sort of discourse. He was painfully aware of how far from fluency these noises fell, but Willy always let him have his say, and in the end that was all that mattered. Mr. Bones was free to put in his two cents, and whenever he did so his master would give him his full attention, and to look at Willy's face as he watched his friend struggle to make like a member of the human tribe, you would have sworn that he was hanging on every word.

That gloomy Sunday in Baltimore, however, Mr. Bones kept his mouth shut. They were down to their last days together, perhaps even their last hours, and this was no time to indulge in long speeches and loopy contortions, no time for the old shenanigans. Certain situations called for tact and discipline, and in their present dire straits it would be far better to hold his tongue and behave like a good, loyal dog. He let Willy snap the leash on to his collar without protest. He didn't whine about not having eaten in the past thirty-six hours; he didn't sniff the air for female scents; he didn't stop to pee on every lamppost and fire hydrant. He simply ambled along beside Willy, following his master as they searched the empty avenues for 316 Calvert Street.

Mr. Bones had nothing against Baltimore per se. It smelled no worse than any other city they'd camped in over the years, but even though he understood the purpose of the trip, it grieved him to think that a man could choose to spend his last moments on earth in a place he'd never been to before. A dog would never commit such a blunder. He would make his peace with the world and then see to it that he gave up the ghost on familiar ground. But Willy still had two things

to accomplish before he died, and with character-
istic stubbornness he'd gotten it into his head
that there was only one person who could help
him. The name of that person was Bea Swanson,
and since said Bea Swanson was last known to be
living in Baltimore, they had come to Baltimore
to find her. All well and good, but unless Willy's
plan did what it was supposed to do, Mr. Bones
would be marooned in this city of crab cakes and
marble steps, and what was he going to do then?
A phone call would have done the job in half a
minute, but Willy had a philosophical aversion to
using the telephone for important business. He
would rather walk for days on end than pick up
one of those contraptions and talk to someone he
couldn't see. So here they were two hundred
miles later, wandering around the streets of Baltimore without a map, looking for an address that
might or might not exist.

Of the two things Willy still hoped to accomplish before he died, neither one took precedence
over the other. Each was all important to him,
and since time had grown too short to think of
tackling them separately, he had come up with
what he referred to as the Chesapeake Gambit:
an eleventh-hour ploy to kill both birds with one
stone. The first has already been discussed in the
previous paragraphs: to find new digs for his

furry companion. The second was to wrap up his own affairs and make sure that his manuscripts were left in good hands. At that moment, his life's work was crammed into a rental locker at the Greyhound bus terminal on Fayette Street, two and a half blocks north of where he and Mr. Bones were standing. The key was in his pocket, and unless he found someone worthy enough to entrust with that key, every word he had ever written would be destroyed, disposed of as so much unclaimed baggage.

In the twenty-three years since he'd taken on the surname of Christmas, Willy had filled the pages of seventy-four notebooks with his writings. These included poems, stories, essays, diary entries, epigrams, autobiographical musings, and the first eighteen hundred lines of an epic-in-progress, *Vagabond Days*. The majority of these works had been composed at the kitchen table of his mother's apartment in Brooklyn, but since her death four years ago he'd been forced to write in the open air, often battling the elements in public parks and dusty alleyways as he struggled to get his thoughts down on paper. In his secret heart of hearts, Willy had no delusions about himself. He knew that he was a troubled soul and not fit for this world, but he also knew that much good work was buried in those notebooks, and on that score at least he could hold his head high. Maybe if he had been more scrupulous about taking his medication, or maybe if his body had been a bit stronger, or maybe if he hadn't been so fond of malts and spirits and the hubbub of bars, he might have done even more good work. That was perfectly possible, but it was too late to dwell on regrets and errors now. Willy had written the last sentence he would ever write, and there were no more than a few ticks left in the clock. The words in the locker were all he had to show for himself. If the words vanished, it would be as if he had never lived.

That was where Bea Swanson entered the picture. Willy knew it was a stab in the dark, but if and when he managed to find her, he was convinced that she would move heaven and earth to help him. Once upon a time, back when the world was still young, Mrs. Swanson had been his high-school English teacher, and if not for her it was doubtful that he ever would have found the courage to think of himself as a writer. He was still William Gurevitch in those days, a scrawny sixteen-year-old boy with a passion for books and beebop jazz, and she had taken him under her wing and lavished his early work with praise that was so excessive, so far out of proportion to its true merit, that he began to think of himself as the next great hope of American literature. Whether she was right or wrong to do so is not the question, for results are less important at that stage than promise, and Mrs. Swanson had recognized his talent, she'd seen the spark in his fledgling soul, and no one can ever amount to anything in this life without someone else to believe in him. That's a proven fact, and while the rest of the junior class at Midwood High saw Mrs. Swanson as a squat, fortyish woman with blubbery arms that bounced and wiggled whenever she wrote on the blackboard, Willy thought she was beautiful, an angel who had come down from heaven and taken on a human form.

By the time school started again in the fall, however, Mrs. Swanson was gone. Her husband had been offered a new job in Baltimore, and since Mrs. Swanson was not only a teacher but a wife, what choice did she have but to leave Brooklyn and go where Mr. Swanson went? It was a tough blow for Willy to absorb, but it could have been worse, for even though his mentor was far away, she did not forget him. Over the next several years, Mrs. Swanson kept up a lively correspondence with her young friend, continuing to read and comment on the manuscripts he sent her, to remember his birthday with gifts of old Charlie Parker records, and to suggest little magazines where he could begin submitting his work. The gushing, rhapsodic letter of recommendation she wrote for him in his senior year helped clinch a full scholarship for Willy at Columbia. Mrs. Swanson was his muse, his protector and good-luck charm all rolled into one, and at that point in Willy's life, the sky was definitely the limit. But then came the schizo flip-out of 1968, the mad fandango of truth or consequences on a high-voltage tension wire. They shut him up in a hospital, and after six months of shock treatment and psychopharmacological therapy, he was never quite the same again. Willy had joined the ranks of the walking wounded, and even though he continued to churn out his poems and stories, to go on writing in both sickness and in health, he rarely got around to answering Mrs. Swanson's letters. The reasons were unimportant. Perhaps Willy was embarrassed to stay in touch with her. Perhaps he was distracted, preoccupied with other business. Perhaps he had lost faith in the US Postal Service and no longer trusted the mail carriers not to snoop inside the letters they delivered. One way or the other, his once voluminous exchanges with Mrs. Swanson dwindled to almost nothing. For a year or two, they consisted of the odd, desultory postcard, then the store-bought Christmas greeting, and then, by 1976, they had stopped altogether. Since that time, not one syllable of communication had passed between them.

Mr. Bones knew all this, and that was precisely what worried him. Seventeen years had gone by. Gerald Ford had been President back then, for Chrissakes, and he himself would not be whelped for another decade. Who was Willy trying to kid? Think of all the things that can happen in that time. Think of the changes that can occur in seventeen hours or seventeen minutes – let alone in seventeen years. At the very least, Mrs. Swanson had probably moved to another address. The old girl would be pushing seventy by now, and if she wasn't senile or living in a trailer park in Florida, there was a better than even chance that she was dead. Willy had admitted as much when they hit the streets of Baltimore that morning, but what the fuck, he'd said, it was their one and only shot, and since life was a gamble anyway, why not go for broke?

Ah, Willy. He had told so many stories, had talked in so many different voices, had spoken out of so many sides of his mouth at once that Mr. Bones had no idea what to believe anymore. What was true, what was false? It was difficult to know when dealing with a character as complex and fanciful as Willy G. Christmas. Mr. Bones could vouch for the things he'd seen with his own eyes, the events he'd experienced in his own flesh, but he and Willy had been together for only seven years, and the facts concerning the previous thirty-eight were more or less up for grabs. If Mr. Bones hadn't spent his puppyhood living under the same roof with Willy's mother, the whole story would have been shrouded in darkness, but by listening to Mrs. Gurevitch and measuring her statements against her son's, Mr. Bones had managed to stitch together a reasonably coherent portrait of what Willy's world had looked like before he came into it. A thousand details were lacking. A thousand others were muddled in confusion, but Mr. Bones had a sense of the drift, a feeling for what its shape both was and wasn't.

It wasn't rich, for example, and it wasn't cheerful, and more often than not the air in the apartment had been tinged with sourness and desperation. Considering what the family had been through before it landed in America, it was probably a miracle that David Gurevitch and Ida Perlmutter managed to produce a son in the first place. Of the seven children born to Willy's grandparents in Warsaw and Lodz between 1910 and 1921, they were the only two to survive the war. They alone did not have numbers tattooed on their forearms, they alone were granted the luck to escape. But that didn't mean they had an easy time of it, and Mr. Bones had heard enough stories to make his fur tingle. There were the ten days they spent hiding in an attic crawl space in Warsaw. There was the month-long walk from Paris to the Free Zone in the south, sleeping in haylofts and stealing eggs to stay alive. There was the refugee internment camp in Mende, the money spent on bribes for safe conducts, the four months of bureaucratic hell in Marseille as they waited for their Spanish transit visas. Then came the long coma of immobility in Lisbon, the still-born son Ida delivered in 1944, the two years of looking out at the Atlantic as the war dragged on and their money ebbed away. By the time Willy's parents arrived in Brooklyn in 1946, it wasn't a new life they were starting so much as a posthumous life, an interval between two deaths. Willy's father, once a clever young lawyer in Poland, begged a job from a distant cousin and spent the next thirteen years riding the Seventh Avenue IRT to a button-manufacturing firm on West Twenty-eighth Street. For the first year, Willy's mother supplemented their income by giving piano lessons to young Jewish brats in the apartment, but that ended one morning in November of 1947 when Willy poked his little face out from between her legs and unexpectedly refused to stop breathing.

He grew up American, a Brooklyn boy who played stickball in the streets, read *Mad Magazine* under the covers at night, and listened to Buddy Holly and the Big Bopper. Neither one of his parents could fathom such things, but that was just as well as far as Willy was concerned, since his great goal in life at that stage was to convince himself that his mother and father were not his real parents. He found them alien, wholly embarrassing creatures, a pair of sore thumbs with their Polish accents and stilted foreign ways, and without really having to think about it he understood that his only hope of survival lay in resisting them at every turn. When his father dropped dead from a heart attack at forty-nine, Willy's sorrow was mitigated by a secret sense of relief. Already at twelve, just barely on the brink of adolescence, he had formulated his lifelong philosophy of embracing trouble wherever he could find it. The more wretched your life was, the closer you were to the truth, to the gritty nub of existence, and what could be more terrible than losing your old man six weeks after your twelfth birthday? It marked you as a tragic figure, disqualified you from the rat race of vain hopes and sentimental illusions, bestowed on you an aura of legitimate suffering. But the fact was that Willy didn't suffer much. His father had always been a riddle to him, a man prone to weeklong silences and sudden outbursts of rage, and more than once he had slapped down Willy for the smallest, most trifling infraction. No, it wasn't hard to adjust to life without that bag of explosives. It didn't take any effort at all.

Or so reckoned the good Herr Doktor Bones. Ignore his opinion if you will, but who else are you prepared to trust? After listening to these stories for the past seven years, had he not earned the right to be called the world's leading authority on the subject?

That left Willy alone with his mother. She was hardly anyone's idea of a good time, but at least she kept her hands to herself and showed him considerable amounts of affection, enough warmth of heart to counterbalance the periods when she nagged him and harangued him and got on his nerves. By and large, Willy tried to be a good son. At those rare moments when he was able to stop thinking about himself, he even made a conscious effort to be nice to her. If they had their differences, they were less a result of personal animosity than of starkly opposing world views. From hard-won experience, Mrs. Gurevitch knew that the world was out to get her, and she lived her life accordingly, doing everything in her power to stay clear of harm's way. Willy also knew that the world was out to get him, but unlike his mother he had no qualms about fighting back. The difference was not that one was a pessimist and the other an optimist, it was that one's pessimism had led to an ethos of fear, and the other's pessimism had led to a noisy, fractious disdain for Everything-That-Was. One shrank, the other flailed. One toed the line, the other crossed it out. Much of the time they were at loggerheads, and because Willy found it so easy to shock his mother, he rarely wasted an opportunity to provoke an argument. If only she'd had the wit to back off a little, he probably wouldn't have been so insistent about making his points. Her antagonism inspired him, pushed him into ever more extreme positions, and by the time he was ready to leave the house and go off to college, he had indelibly cast himself in his chosen role: as malcontent, as rebel, as outlaw poet prowling the gutters of a ruined world.

Lord knows how many drugs that boy ingested in the two and a half years he spent on Morningside Heights. Name an illegal substance, and Willy either smoked it or snorted it or shot it into his veins. It's one thing to walk around pretending you're the second coming of François

Villon, but feed an unstable young man enough toxic confections to fill a dump site in the Jersey Meadowlands, and his body chemistry is bound to be altered. Sooner or later, Willy might have cracked up anyway, but who would argue that the psychedelic free-for-all of his student days didn't accelerate the process? When his roommate walked in on him one afternoon in the middle of his junior year and found Willy buck naked on the floor – chanting names from the Manhattan phone book and eating a bowl of his own excrement – the academic career of Mr. Bones's future master came to an abrupt and permanent end.

The loony bin followed, and then Willy returned to his mother's apartment on Glenwood Avenue. It wasn't the ideal place for him to live, perhaps, but where else could a burnout like poor Willy go? For the first six months, not much good came of the arrangement. Other than Willy's switch from drugs to alcohol, things were essentially the same as they had been. The same tensions, the same conflicts, the same misunderstandings. Then, out of the blue, in late December 1969, Willy had the vision that changed everything, the mystical encounter with blessedness that turned him inside out and set his life on an entirely different course.

It was two-thirty in the morning. His mother had gone to bed several hours before, and Willy was parked on the living-room sofa with a pack of Luckies and a bottle of bourbon, watching television out of the corner of one eye. Television was a new habit for him, a by-product of his recent stay in the hospital. He wasn't particularly interested in the images on the screen, but he enjoyed having the hum and glow of the tube in the background and found comfort in the gray-blue shadows it cast on the walls. The *Late Late Show* was on just then (something to do with gigantic grasshoppers devouring the citizens of Sacramento, California), but most of the airtime had been given over to chintzy exhortations on behalf of miracle breakthrough products: knives that never went dull, lightbulbs that never burned out, secret-formula lotions that removed the curse of baldness. Yak yak yak, Willy muttered to himself, it's the same old suds and blather. Just as he was about to stand up and turn off the television, however, a new commercial came on, and there was Santa Claus popping out of someone's fireplace in what looked like a suburban living room in Massapequa, Long Island. Given that Christmas was just around the corner, Willy had grown used to commercials that featured actors dressed up as Santa Claus. But this one was better than most – a roly-poly guy with rosy cheeks and an honest-to-goodness white beard. Willy paused to watch the beginning of the spiel, fully expecting to hear something about rug shampoos or burglar alarms, when all of a sudden Santa uttered the words that would change his destiny.

"William Gurevitch," Santa said. "Yes, William Gurevitch of Brooklyn, New York, I'm talking to you."

Willy had drunk only half a bottle that night, and it had been eight months since his last full-blown hallucination. Nobody was going to trick him into swallowing this garbage. He knew the difference between reality and make-believe, and if Santa Claus was talking to him from his mother's television set, that could only mean he was a lot drunker than he supposed.

"Fuck you, mister," Willy said, and without giving the matter another thought, he clicked off the machine.

Unfortunately, he wasn't able to leave things as they were. Because he was curious, or because he wanted to make sure he wasn't having another breakdown, Willy decided it would be all right if he turned the television back on – just for a peek, a last little peek. It wasn't going to hurt anyone, was it? Better to learn the truth now than to walk around with that sack of Yuletide shit preying on his mind for the next forty years.

And lo and behold, there he was again. There was Santa bloody Claus, wagging his finger at Willy and shaking his head with a sad, disappointed look in his eyes. When he opened his mouth and started to talk (picking up precisely where he had left off ten seconds earlier), Willy didn't know whether he should burst out laughing or jump through the window. It was happening, folks. What could not happen was happening, and right then and there Willy knew that nothing in the world would ever look the same to him again.

"That wasn't nice, William," Santa said. "I'm here to help you, but we're never going to get anywhere if you don't give me a chance to talk. Do you follow me, son?"

The question seemed to call for a response, but Willy hesitated. Listening to this clown was bad enough. Did he really want to make things worse by talking back to him?

"William!" Santa said. His voice was stern and reproachful, and it contained the power of a personality that was not to be trifled with. If Willy was ever going to squirm out of this nightmare, his only hope would be to play along.

"Yeah, boss," he mumbled, "I read you loud and clear."

The fat man smiled. Then, very slowly, the camera moved in on him for a close-up. For the next several seconds Santa stood there stroking his beard, apparently lost in thought.

"Do you know who I am?" he finally said.

"I know who you look like," Willy said, "but that doesn't mean I know who you are. At first I thought you were some asshole actor. Then I thought maybe you were that genie in the bottle. Now I don't have a clue."

"The thing I look like is the thing I am."

"Sure, pal, and I'm Haile Selassie's brother-in-law."

"Santa Claus, William. A.k.a. Saint Nick. Father Christmas himself. The only force for good left in the world."

"Santa, huh? And you wouldn't happen to spell that S–A–N–T–A, would you?"

"Yes, I would. That's exactly how I'd spell it."

"That's what I figured. Now rearrange the letters a little bit, and what do you have? S–A–T–A–N, that's what. You're the goddamn devil, grandpa, and the only place you exist is in my mind."

Notice how Willy struggled against the apparition, how determined he was to thwart its charms. He wasn't some pea-brained psycho who let figments and specters push him around. He wanted no part of this one, and the disgust he felt, the downright hostility he expressed whenever he recalled the first moments of the encounter, was precisely what convinced Mr. Bones that it was true, that Willy had experienced an authentic vision and was not making the story up. To hear him tell it, the situation was a scandal, an insult to his intelligence, and merely having to look at that bovine lump of clichés brought his blood to a boil. Let someone else make with the ho-ho stuff. Christmas was a fraud, a season for quick bucks and ringing cash registers, and as the symbol of that season, as the very essence of the whole consumerist shebang, Santa was the biggest fake of them all.

But this Santa was no fake, and he was no devil in disguise. He was the true Father Christmas, the one and only Lord of the Elves and Spirits, and the message he'd come to preach was one of goodness, generosity, and self-sacrifice. This unlikeliest of fictions, this contradiction of everything Willy stood for, this absurd display of hokum in the red jacket and the fur-fringed boots – yes, Santa Claus in all his Madison Avenue glory – had sprung forth from the depths of Television Land to debunk the certitudes of Willy's skepticism and put his soul back together again. It was as simple as that. If anyone was a fraud, Santa said, it was Willy, and then he let him have it in no uncertain terms, lecturing the frightened and bewildered boy for the better part of an hour. He called him a sham, a poseur, and a no-talent hack. Then he upped the ante and called him a zero, a douche bag, a dunderhead, and little by little he broke down the wall of Willy's defenses and made him see the light. Willy was on the floor by then, weeping his eyes out as he begged for mercy and promised to mend his ways. Christmas was real, he learned, and there would be no truth or happiness for him until he began to embrace its spirit. That would be his mission in life from now on: to embody the message of Christmas every day of the year, to ask nothing from the world and give it only love in return.

In other words, Willy decided to turn himself into a saint.

And so it happened that William Gurevitch concluded his business on this earth, and from his flesh a new man named Willy G. Christmas was born. To celebrate the event, Willy scuttled off to Manhattan the next morning and had himself tattooed with a picture of Santa Claus on his right arm. It was a painful ordeal, but Willy suffered the needles gladly, triumphant in the knowledge that he now bore a visible sign of his transformation and would carry its mark with him for ever.

Alas, when he returned to Brooklyn and proudly showed his mother this new ornament, Mrs. Gurevitch went wild, erupting in a tantrum of tears and angry disbelief. It wasn't just the idea of the tattoo that bent her out of shape (although that was part of it, given that tattooing was proscribed by Jewish law – and given what role the tattooing of Jewish skin had played in her life-time), it was what *this particular tattoo* represented, and in that Mrs. Gurevitch saw the three-color Santa Claus on Willy's arm as a token of betrayal and incurable madness, her outburst at that moment was perhaps understandable. Until then, she had managed to delude herself into thinking that her son would make a full recovery. She blamed his condition on the drugs, and once the noxious residues were flushed out of his system and his blood count returned to normal, she felt it would only be a matter of time before he turned off the television set and went back to college. But not any more. One glance at the tattoo, and all those vain hopes and false expectations shattered at her feet like so much glass. Santa Claus was from the other side. He belonged to the Presbyterians and the Roman

Catholics, to the Jesus-worshippers and Jew-haters, to Hitler and all the rest of them. The *goyim* had taken hold of Willy's brain, and once they crawled inside you, they never let go. Christmas was only the first step. Easter was just a few months down the road, and then they'd drag out those crosses of theirs and start talking about murder, and before long the storm troopers would be breaking down the door. She saw the picture of Santa Claus emblazoned on her son's arm, but as far as she was concerned, it might just as well have been a swastika.

Willy was frankly perplexed. He hadn't meant any harm, and in his present blissful state of remorse and conversion, the last thing he wanted was to offend his mother. But talk and explain as he did, she refused to listen. She shrieked at him and called him a Nazi, and when he persisted in trying to make her understand that Santa Claus was an incarnation of the Buddha, a holy being whose message to the world was one of merciful love and compassion, she threatened to send him back to the hospital that very afternoon. This brought to mind a sentence that Willy had heard from a fellow patient at Saint Luke's – "I'd rather have a bottle in front of me than a frontal lobotomy" – and suddenly he knew what was in store for him if he let his mother have her way. So, rather than go on beating a dead horse, he climbed into his overcoat and left the apartment, heading in a beeline for God knows where.

Thus began a pattern that continued for the next umpteen years. Willy would stay with his mother for several months, then leave for several months, then come back. The first departure was probably the most dramatic, if only because Willy still had everything to learn about the wandering life. He was gone for just a short spell, and although Mr. Bones was never quite certain what Willy meant by *short*, whatever happened to his master during the weeks or months he was away proved to him that he had found his true calling. "Don't tell me that two and two is four," Willy said to his mother when he returned to Brooklyn. "How do we know that two is two? That's the real question."

The next day, he sat down and started writing again. It was the first time he'd picked up a pen since before the hospital, and the words poured out of him like water gushing from a broken pipe. Willy G. Christmas proved to be a better and more inspired poet than William Gurevitch had ever been, and what his early efforts lacked in originality, they made up for in hell-bent enthusiasm. *Thirty-three Rules to Live By* was a good example. Its opening lines read as follows:

Throw yourself into the arms of the world
And the air will hold you. Hold back
And the world will jump you from behind.
Go for broke down the highway of bones.
Follow the music of your steps, and when the lights
  go out
Don't whistle – sing.
If you keep your eyes open, you'll always be lost.
Give away your shirt, give away your gold,
Give away your shoes to the first stranger you see.
Much will come of nothing
If you dance the jitterbug waltz . . .

Literary pursuits were one thing, but how you conducted yourself in the world was quite another. Willy's poems might have changed, but that still didn't answer the question about whether Willy himself had changed. Did he actually become a new person, or was the plunge into sainthood no more than a passing impulse? Had he boondoggled himself into an untenable position, or was there something more to be said about his rebirth than the tattoo on his right biceps and the ridiculous moniker he took such pleasure in using? An honest answer would be yes and no, perhaps, a little of both. For Willy was weak, and Willy was often belligerent, and Willy was prone to forget things. Mental mishaps dogged him, and whenever the pinball machine in his head speeded up and went tilt, all bets were off. How could a man of his ilk propose to don the mantle of purity? Not only was he an incipient lush, and not only was he a bred-in-the-bone liar with a strong paranoiac bent, he was too damn funny for his own good. Once Willy started in with the jokes, Santa Claus burst into flames, and the whole hearts-and-flowers act burned to the ground with him.

Still and all, it would be wrong to say that he didn't try, and in that trying hung a large part of the story. Even if Willy didn't always live up to his expectations for himself, at least he had a model for how he wanted to behave. At those rare moments when he was able to focus his thoughts and curb his excesses in the beverage department, Willy demonstrated that no act of courage or generosity was beyond him. In 1972, for example, at no small risk to himself, he rescued a four-year-old girl from drowning. In 1976, he came to the defense of an eighty-one-year-old man who was being mugged on West Forty-third Street in New York – and for his pains received a knife wound in his shoulder and a bullet in his leg. More than once he gave his last dollar to a friend down on his luck, he let the lovelorn and the heartsick cry on his shoulder, and over the years he talked one man and two women out of suicide. There were fine things in Willy's soul, and whenever he let them come out, you forgot the other things that were in there as well. Yes, he was a bedraggled, demented pain in the ass, but when all was right in his head, Willy was one in a million, and everyone who crossed paths with him knew it.

Whenever he talked to Mr. Bones about those early years, Willy tended to dwell on the good memories and ignore the bad. But who could blame him for sentimentalizing the past? We all do it, dogs and people alike, and in 1970 Willy had been nowhere if not in the pink of youth. His health was as robust as it would ever be, his teeth were intact, and to top it off he had money in the bank. A small sum had been set aside for him from his father's life-insurance policy, and when he came into this money on his twenty-first birthday, he was kept in pocket change for close to a decade. But above and beyond the boon of money and youth, there was the historical moment, the times themselves, the spirit abroad in the land when Willy set forth on his career of vagabondage. The country was crawling with dropouts and runaway children, with long-haired neo-visionaries, dysfunctional anarchists, and doped-up misfits. For all the oddness he demonstrated in his own right, Willy hardly stood out among them. He was just one more weirdo on the Amerikan scene, and wherever his travels happened to take him – be it Pittsburgh or Plattsburgh, Pocatello or Boca Raton – he managed to latch on to like-minded souls for company. Or so he said, and in the long run Mr. Bones saw no reason to doubt him.

Not that it would have made any difference if he had. The dog had lived long enough to know that good stories were not necessarily true stories, and whether he chose to believe the stories Willy told about himself or not was less important than the fact that Willy had done what he had done, and the years had passed. That was the essential thing, wasn't it? The years, the number of years it took to go from being young to not-so-young, and all the while to watch the world change around you. By the time Mr. Bones crept forth from his mother's womb, Willy's salad days were but a dim memory, a pile of compost moldering in a vacant lot. The runaways had crawled back home to mom and dad; the pot-heads had traded in their love beads for paisley ties; the war was over. But Willy was still Willy, the boffo rhymester and self-appointed bearer of Santa's message, your basic sorry excuse rigged out in the filthy duds of tramphood. The passage of time had not treated the poet kindly, and he didn't blend in so well anymore. He stank and drooled, he rubbed people the wrong way, and what with the bullet wounds and the knife wounds and the general deterioration of his physical self, he'd lost his quickness, his heretofore astonishing knack for slithering out of trouble. Strangers robbed him and beat him up. They kicked him while he slept, they set his books on fire, they took advantage of his aches and pains. After one such encounter landed him in the hospital with blurred vision and a fractured arm, he realized that he couldn't go on without some kind of protection. He thought of a gun, but weapons were abhorrent to him, and so he settled on the next best thing known to man: a bodyguard with four legs.

Mrs. Gurevitch was less than thrilled, but Willy put his foot down and got his way. So the young Mr. Bones was torn from his mother and five siblings at the North Shore Animal Shelter and moved to Glenwood Avenue in Brooklyn. To be perfectly honest, he didn't remember much about those early days. Ingloosh was still virgin territory to him back then, and what with Mrs. Gurevitch's bizarrely mangled locutions and Willy's penchant for talking in different voices (Gabby Hayes one minute, Louis Armstrong the next; Groucho Marx in the morning, Maurice

Chevalier at night), it took several months to get the hang of it. In the meantime, there were the agonies of puppyhood: the struggles with bladder and bowel control, the newspapers on the kitchen floor, the snout-whacks from Mrs. Gurevitch every time the pee dribbled out of him. She was a crotchety old complainer, that one, and if not for Willy's gentle hands and soothing endearments, life in that apartment would have been no picnic. Winter was upon them, and with everything ice and stinging salt pellets on the streets below, he spent ninety-eight percent of his time indoors, either sitting at Willy's feet as the poet cranked out his latest masterpiece or exploring the nooks and crevices of his new home. The apartment consisted of four and a half rooms, and by the time spring came Mr. Bones was familiar with every stick of furniture, every blot on the rugs, every gash in the linoleum. He knew the smell of Mrs. Gurevitch's slippers and the smell of Willy's underpants. He knew the difference between the doorbell and the telephone, could distinguish between the sound of jangling keys and the clatter of pills in a plastic vial, and before long he was on a first-name basis with every cockroach who lived in the cupboard under the kitchen sink. It was a dull, circumscribed routine, but how was Mr. Bones to know that? He was no more than a lame-brained pup, a nincompoop with floppy paws who ran after his own tail and chomped on his own shit, and if this was the only life he'd ever tasted, who was he to judge whether it was rich or poor in the stuff that makes life worth living?

Was that little mutt in for a surprise! When the weather at last turned warm and the flowers unfurled their buds, he learned that Willy was more than just a pencil-pushing homebody and professional jerk-off artist. His master was a man with the heart of a dog. He was a rambler, a rough-and-ready soldier of fortune, a one-of-a-kind two-leg who improvised the rules as he went along. They simply upped and left one morning in the middle of April, launched out into the great beyond, and saw neither hide nor hair of Brooklyn until the day before Halloween. Could a dog ask for more than that? As far as Mr. Bones was concerned, he was the luckiest creature on the face of the earth.

There were the winter hibernations, of course, the returns to the ancestral home, and with them the inevitable drawbacks to life indoors: the long months of hissing steam radiators, the infernal ruckus of vacuum cleaners and Waring blenders, the tedium of canned food. Once Mr. Bones caught on to the rhythm, however, he had little cause for complaint. It was cold out there, after all, and the apartment had Willy in it, and how bad could life be if he and his master were together? Even Mrs. Gurevitch eventually seemed to come round. Once the housebreaking issue was resolved, he noticed a distinct softening in her attitude toward him, and though she continued to grumble about the hairs he deposited throughout her domain, he understood that her heart was not fully in it. Sometimes she would even let him sit beside her on the living-room sofa, softly stroking his head with one hand as she flipped through her magazine with the other, and more than once she actually confided in him, unburdening herself of assorted worries in regard to her wayward, benighted son. What a sorrow he was to her, and what a sad thing it was that such a fine boy should be so screwed up in the head. But half a son was better than no son, *farshtaist?*, and what choice did she have but to go on loving him and hope that things turned out for the best? They'd never allow him to be buried in a Jewish cemetery – not with that funny business on his arm, they wouldn't – and just knowing that he wouldn't be laid to rest beside his mother and father was another sorrow, another torment that preyed on her mind, but life was for the living, wasn't it?, and thank God they were both in good health – touch wood – or at least not so bad, all things considered, and that in itself was a blessing, something to be thankful for, and you couldn't buy that at the five-and-dime, could you?, they didn't have commercials for that on TV. Color, black-and-white, it didn't matter what kind of set you had. Life wasn't for sale, and once you found yourself at death's door, all the noodles in China weren't going to stop that door from opening.

As Mr. Bones discovered, the differences between Mrs. Gurevitch and her son were much smaller than he had at first supposed. It was true that they often disagreed, and it was true that their smells had nothing in common – the one being all dirt and male sweat, the other a mélange of lilac soaps, Pond's facial cream, and spearmint denture paste – but when it came to talking, this sixty-eight-year-old *Mom-san* could hold her own with anyone, and once she let fly with one of her interminable monologues, you quickly understood why her offspring had turned into such a champion chatterbox. The subjects they talked about might have been different, but their styles were essentially the same: lurching, nonstop runs of free association, numerous asides and parenthetical remarks, and a full repertoire of extraverbal effects, replete with everything from clicks to chortles to deep glottal gasps. From Willy, Mr. Bones learned about humor, irony, and metaphorical abundance. From *Mom-san*, he learned important lessons about what it meant to be alive. She taught him about anxiety and tsuris, about bearing the weight of the world on your shoulders, and – most important of all – about the benefits of an occasional good cry.

As he trudged along beside his master that dreary Sunday in Baltimore, Mr. Bones found it odd that he should be thinking about these things now. Why hark back to Mrs. Gurevitch?, he wondered. Why recall the tedium of the Brooklyn winters when there were so many fuller and more buoyant memories to contemplate? Albuquerque, for example, and their blissful sojourn in that abandoned bed factory two years ago. Or Greta, the voluptuous she-hound he'd romped with for ten nights running in a cornfield outside of Iowa City. Or that nutty afternoon in Berkeley four summers ago when Willy had sold eighty-six xeroxed copies of a single poem on Telegraph Avenue for a dollar a piece. It would have done him a world of good to be able to relive some of those things now, to be back somewhere with his master before the cough began – even last year, even nine or ten months ago, yes, maybe even hanging out with that tubby broad Willy had shacked up with for a while – Wanda, Wendy, whatever her name was – the girl who lived out of the back of her station wagon in Denver and liked to feed him hard-boiled eggs. She was a pistol, that one, a bawdy sack of blubber and booze, always laughing too much, always tickling him on the soft part of his belly and then, whenever his pink doggy dick came popping out of its sheath (not that Mr. Bones objected, mind you), roaring with even more laughter, so much laughter that her face would turn fifteen shades of purple, and so often was this little comedy repeated during the short time they spent with her that he had only to hear the word *Denver* now for Wanda's laugh to start ringing in his ears again. That was *Denver* for him, just as *Chicago* was a bus splashing through a rain puddle on Michigan Avenue. Just as *Tampa* was a wall of light shimmering up from the asphalt one August afternoon. Just as *Tucson* was a hot wind blowing off the desert, bearing with it the scent of juniper leaves and sagebrush, the sudden, unearthly plenitude of the vacant air.

One by one, he tried to attach himself to these memories, to inhabit them for a few more moments as they flitted past him, but it was no use. He kept going back to the Brooklyn apartment, to the languors of those cold-weather confinements, to *Mom-san* padding around the rooms in her fluffy white slippers. There was nothing to do but stay there, he realized, and as he finally gave in to the force of those endless days and nights, he understood that he had returned to Glenwood Avenue because Mrs. Gurevitch was dead. She had left this world, just as her son was about to leave it, and by rehearsing that earlier death, he was no doubt preparing himself for the next one, the death of deaths, which was destined to turn the world upside down, perhaps even destroy it entirely.

Winter had always been the season of poetic labor. Willy kept nocturnal hours when he was at home, and most often he would start his day's work just after his mother went to bed. Life on the road did not allow for the rigors of composition. The pace was too hurried, the spirit too peripatetic, the distractions too continuous for anything but an infrequent jotting, the odd note or phrase dashed off on a paper napkin. During the months he spent in Brooklyn, however, Willy generally put in three or four hours a night at the kitchen table, scratching out his verses into 8½" by 11" spiral notebooks. At least that was the case when he wasn't off on a binge somewhere, or too down in the dumps, or stymied by a lack of inspiration. He sometimes muttered to himself as he wrote, sounding out the words as he put them down on paper, and sometimes he even went so far as to laugh or growl or pound his fist on the table. At first, Mr. Bones assumed these noises were directed at him, but once he learned that carryings-on of this sort were part of the creative process, he would content himself with curling up under the table and dozing at his master's feet, waiting for the moment when the night's work was done and he would be taken outside to empty his bladder.

Still, it hadn't been all slump and torpor, had it? Even in Brooklyn there had been some bright spots, some deviations from the literary grind. Go back thirty-eight years on the dog calendar, for example, and there was the Symphony of Smells, that unique and shining chapter in the annals of Willydom, when for one whole winter there were no words at all. Yes, that surely was a time, Mr. Bones said to himself, a most beautiful and crazy time, and to recollect it now sent a warm glow of nostalgia coursing through his blood. Had he been capable of smiling, he would have smiled at that moment. Had he been capable of shedding tears, he would have shed tears. Indeed, if such a thing were possible, he would have been laughing and crying at the same time –

both celebrating and mourning his beloved master, who was soon to be no more.

The Symphony went back to the early days of their life together. They had left Brooklyn twice, had returned to Brooklyn twice, and in that time Willy had developed the keenest, most ardent affection for his four-legged friend. Not only did he feel protected now, and not only was he glad to have someone to talk to, and not only did it comfort him to have a warm body to curl up against at night, but after living with the dog at such close quarters for so many months, Willy had judged him to be wholly and incorruptibly good. It wasn't just that he knew that Mr. Bones had a soul. He knew that soul to be better than other souls, and the more he saw of it, the more refinement and nobility of spirit he found there. Was Mr. Bones an angel trapped in the flesh of a dog? Willy thought so. After eighteen months of the most intimate, clear-eyed observations, he felt certain of it. How else to interpret the celestial pun that echoed in his mind night and day? To decode the message, all you had to do was hold it up to a mirror. Could anything be more obvious? Just turn around the letters of the word *dog*, and what did you have? The truth, that's what. The lowest being contained within his name the power of the highest being, the almighty artificer of all things. Was that why the dog had been sent to him? Was Mr. Bones, in fact, the second coming of the force that had delivered Santa Claus to him on that December night in 1969? Perhaps. And then again, perhaps not. To anyone else, the matter would have been open to debate. To Willy – precisely because he was Willy – it wasn't.

Still and all, Mr. Bones was a dog. From the tip of his tail to the end of his snout, he was a pure example of *Canis familiaris*, and whatever divine presence he might have harbored within his skin, he was first and foremost the thing he appeared to be. Mr. Bow Wow, Monsieur Woof Woof, Sir Cur. As one wag neatly put it to Willy in a Chicago bar four or five summers back: "You want to know what a dog's philosophy of life is, pal? I'll tell you what it is. Just one sentence: 'If you can't eat it or screw it, piss on it.'"

Willy had no problem with that. Who knew what theological mysteries were at work in a case like this? If God had sent his son down to earth in the form of a man, why shouldn't an angel come down to earth in the form of a dog? Mr. Bones was a dog, and the truth was that Willy took pleasure in that dogness, found no end of delight in watching the spectacle of his confrère's canine habits. Willy had never kept company with an animal before. As a boy, his parents had turned him down every time he'd asked for a pet. Cats, turtles, parakeets, hamsters, goldfish – they would have nothing to do with them. The apartment was too small, they said, or animals stank, or they cost money, or Willy wasn't responsible enough. As a result, until Mr. Bones came into his life, he had never had the opportunity to observe a dog's behavior at close hand, had never even bothered to give the subject much thought. Dogs were no more than dim presences to him, shadowy figures hovering at the edge of consciousness. You avoided the ones who barked at you, you patted the ones who licked you. That was the extent of his knowledge. Two months after his thirty-eighth birthday, all that suddenly changed.

There was so much to absorb, so much evidence to assimilate, decipher, and make sense of that Willy hardly knew where to begin. The wagging tail as opposed to the tail between the legs. The pricked ears as opposed to the flaccid ears. The rolling on to the back, the running in circles, the anus-sniffs and growls, the kangaroo-hops and midair turns, the stalking crouch, the bared teeth, the cocked head, and a hundred other minute particulars, each one an expression of a thought, a feeling a plan, an urge. It was like learning how to speak a new language, Willy found, like stumbling on to a long-lost tribe of primitive men and having to figure out their impenetrable mores and customs. Once he had surmounted the initial barriers, what intrigued him most was the conundrum he referred to as the Eye–Nose Paradox, or the Senses Census. Willy was a man, and therefore he relied chiefly on sight to form his understanding of the world. Mr. Bones was a dog, and therefore he was next to blind. His eyes were useful to him only in that they helped to distinguish shapes, to make out the broad outlines of things, to tell him whether the object or being that loomed up before him was a hazard to be shunned or an ally to be kissed. For true knowledge, for a genuine grasp of reality in all its manifold configurations, only the nose was of any value. Whatever Mr. Bones knew of the world, whatever he had discovered in the way of insights or passions or ideas, he had been led to by his sense of smell. At first, Willy could scarcely believe his eyes. The dog's avidity for smells seemed boundless, and once he had found an odor that interested him, he would clamp his nose over it with such determination, such whole-hog enthusiasm, that everything else in the world would cease to exist. His nostrils were turned into suction tubes, sniffing up scents in the way a vacuum cleaner inhales bits of broken glass, and there were times, many times in fact, when Willy marveled that the sidewalk did not crack apart from the force and fury of Mr. Bones's snout work. Normally the most obliging of creatures, the dog would grow stubborn, distracted, seem to forget his master entirely, and if Willy happened to tug on the leash before Mr. Bones was ready to move on, before he had ingested the full savor of the turd or urine puddle under scrutiny, he would plant his legs to resist the yank, and so unbudgeable did he become, so firmly did he anchor himself to the spot, that Willy often wondered if there wasn't a sac hidden somewhere in his paws that could secrete glue on command.

How not to be fascinated by all this? A dog had roughly two hundred and twenty million scent receptors, whereas a man had but five million, and with a disparity as great as that, it was logical to assume that the world perceived by a dog was quite different from the one perceived by a man. Logic had never been Willy's strength, but in this case he was driven by love as much as by intellectual curiosity, and therefore he stuck with the question with more persistence than usual. What did Mr. Bones experience when he smelled something? And, just as important, why did he smell what he smelled?

Close observation had led Willy to conclude

that there were essentially three categories of interest to Mr. Bones: food, sex, and information about other dogs. A man opens the morning paper to find out what his fellow creatures have been up to; a dog does the same thing with his nose, sniffing trees and lampposts and fireboxes to learn about the doings of the local dog population. Rex, the sharp-fanged Rottweiler, has left his mark on that bush; Molly, the cute cocker spaniel, is in heat; Roger the mutt ate something that didn't agree with him. That much was clear to Willy, a matter beyond dispute. Where things grew complicated was when you tried to understand what the dog was feeling. Was he merely looking out for himself, digesting information in order to keep a leg up on the other dogs, or was there something more to these frantic sniff-fests than simple military tactics? Could pleasure be involved as well? Could a dog with his head buried in a garbage can experience something akin, say, to the heady swoon that comes over a man when he presses his nose against a woman's neck and breathes in a whiff of ninety-dollar-an-ounce French perfume?

It was impossible to know for sure, but Willy tended to think that he did. Why else would it have been so difficult to wrench Mr. Bones away from the site of certain smells? The dog was enjoying himself, that's why. He was in a state of intoxication, lost in a nasal paradise he could not bear to leave. And if, as has already been established, Willy was convinced that Mr. Bones had a soul, did it not stand to reason that a dog of such spiritual inclinations would aspire to loftier things – things not necessarily related to the needs and urgencies of his body, but spiritual things, artistic things, the immaterial hungers of the soul? And if, as all philosophers on the subject have noted, art is a human activity that relies on the senses to reach that soul, did it not also stand to reason that dogs – at least dogs of Mr. Bones's caliber – would have it in them to feel a similar aesthetic impulse? Would they not, in other words, be able to appreciate art? As far as Willy knew, no one had ever thought of this before. Did that make him the first man in recorded history to believe that such a thing was possible? No matter. It was an idea whose time had come. If dogs were beyond the pull of oil paintings and string quartets, who was to say they wouldn't respond to an art based on the sense of smell? Why not an olfactory art? Why not an art for dogs that dealt with the world as dogs knew it?

Thus began the lunatic winter of 1988. Mr. Bones had never seen Willy so excited, so calm, so filled with steadfast energy. For three and a half months he worked on the project to the exclusion of everything else, scarcely bothering to smoke or drink anymore, sleeping only when absolutely compelled to, all but forgetting to write, read, or pick his nose. He drew up plans, made lists, experimented with smells, traced diagrams, built structures out of wood, canvas, cardboard, and plastic. There were so many calculations to be made, so many tests to be run, so many daunting questions to be answered. What was the ideal sequence of smells? How long should a symphony last, and how many smells should it contain? What was the proper shape of the symphony hall? Should it be constructed as a labyrinth, or was a progression of boxes within boxes better suited to a dog's sensibility? Should the dog do the work alone, or should the dog's owner be there to guide him from one stage of the performance to the next? Should each symphony revolve around a single subject – food, for example, or female scents – or should various elements be mixed together? One by one, Willy talked out these problems with Mr. Bones, asked for his opinions, solicited his advice, and begged his indulgence to serve as guinea pig for the numerous trials and errors that followed. The dog had rarely felt so honored, so implicated in the throb of human affairs. Not only did Willy need him, but that need had been inspired by Mr. Bones himself. From his humble origins as a mutt of no particular worth or distinction, he had been turned into the dog of dogs, an exemplar of the whole canine race. Of course he was happy to do his bit, to play along with whatever Willy asked of him. What difference did it make if he didn't fully understand? He was a dog, wasn't he?, and why should he object to sniffing a pile of urine-soaked rags, to pushing his body through a narrow trapdoor, or to crawling through a tunnel whose walls had been smeared with the traces of a meatball-and-spaghetti dinner? It might not have served any purpose, but the truth was that it was fun.

That was what came back to him now: the fun of it, the ongoing rush of Willy's excitement. Forget *Mom-san* and her sarcastic comments. Forget the fact that their laboratory was in the sub-basement of the building, next to the furnace and the sewage pipes, and that they worked on a cold dirt floor. They were collaborating on something important, enduring hardships together in the name of scientific progress. If there was anything to regret sometimes, it was simply the depth of Willy's commitment to what they were doing. He was so consumed by it, so wrapped up in the nuts and bolts of the project, that it became increasingly hard for him to keep things in perspective. One day, he would talk about his invention as if it were a major discovery, a breakthrough on a par with the lightbulb, the airplane, or the computer chip. It would rake in bags of money, he said, turn them into millionaires many times over, and they would never have to worry about anything again. On other days, however, suddenly filled with doubts and uncertainties, he would present arguments to Mr. Bones that were so finely parsed, so hair-splitting in their exactitude, that the dog began to fear for his master's health. Was it perhaps pushing things too far, Willy asked one evening, to include female scents in the orchestration of the symphonies? Wouldn't those smells induce lust in the dog who inhaled them, and wouldn't that undermine their aesthetic aspirations, turning the piece into something pornographic, a kind of smut for dogs? Immediately following that statement, Willy started bending words again, which happened whenever his mind was working at top speed. "Cure porn with corn," he muttered to himself, pacing back and forth across the dirt floor, "pure corn will cure porn." Once Mr. Bones had untangled the knots of the spoonerism, he understood Willy to mean that sentimentality was preferable to sex, at least as far as the symphonies were concerned, and that to remain faithful to the endeavor of bringing aesthetic pleasure to dogs, spiritual longings would have to be emphasized over physical ones. So, after two straight weeks of rubbing his nose in towels and sponges saturated with the aromas of bitches in heat, Mr. Bones was offered a whole new set of instruments: Willy himself, in all his vaporous guises. Dirty socks, undershirts, shoes, handkerchiefs, pants, scarves, hats – anything and everything that bore the scent of his master. Mr. Bones enjoyed these things, just as he had enjoyed the other things. For the fact was that Mr. Bones was a dog, and dogs enjoyed smelling whatever they were given to smell. It was in their nature; it was what they were born to do; it was, as Willy had correctly observed, their calling in life. For once, Mr. Bones was glad that he had not been endowed with the power of human speech. If he had, he would have been forced to tell Willy the truth, and that would have caused him much pain. For a dog, he would have said, for a dog, dear master, the fact is that the whole world is a symphony of smells. Every hour, every minute, every second of his waking life is at once a physical and a spiritual experience. There is no difference between the inner and the outer, nothing to separate the high from the low. It's as if, as if . . .

Just as Mr. Bones was beginning to unfurl this imaginary speech in his head, he was interrupted by the sound of Willy's voice. *Damn*, he heard him say. *Damn, damn*, and *double damn*. Mr. Bones jerked up his head to see what the trouble was. A light rain had begun to fall, a drizzle so faint that Mr. Bones hadn't even felt it landing on his fluffy coat. But little beads of wetness were glistening in Willy's beard, and the master's black T-shirt had already absorbed enough moisture to be showing a fine polka-dotted pattern. This wasn't good. The last thing Willy needed was to get drenched, but if the sky delivered what it seemed to have promised, that's exactly what was going to happen. Mr. Bones perused the clouds over-head. Barring a sudden change of wind, in less than an hour the present feeble raindrops would develop into a full-blown, lusty downpour. Damn, he thought. How much farther to go before they found Calvert Street? They had been stumbling around for the past twenty or thirty minutes, and Bea Swanson's house was still nowhere in sight. If they didn't get there soon, they weren't going to make it. They weren't going to make it, because Willy wouldn't have the strength to go on.

Given their predicament, the last thing Mr.

Bones was expecting just then was that his master would start to laugh. But there it was, rumbling up from the depths of his stomach and bursting forth into the Sunday stillness: the old familiar *haw*. For a moment he thought that maybe Willy was trying to clear his throat, but when the first *haw* was followed by another *haw*, and then another, and still another after that, he could no longer doubt what his ears were telling him.

"Lookee here, ol' bud," Willy said, launching into his best cowboy twang. This was a voice reserved for special occasions, an accent that Willy called upon only when he found himself in the presence of life's grandest, most dizzying ironies. Baffled though he was to hear it now, Mr. Bones tried to take heart from this sudden shift in the emotional weather.

Willy had come to a full stop on the sidewalk. The neighborhood all around them stank of poverty and uncollected garbage, and yet where should they be standing but in front of the loveliest little house Mr. Bones had ever seen, a toy-sized edifice made of red bricks and adorned with slatted green shutters, three green steps, and a brightly painted white door? A plaque was affixed to the wall, and Willy was squinting forward to read what it said, sounding more and more like a Texas ranch hand with each passing second.

"Two-oh-three North Amity Street," he recited. "Residence of Edgar Allan Poe, eighteen-thirty-two to eighteen-thirty-five. Open to the public April to December, Wednesday through Saturday, noon to three forty-five PM."

It sounded like pretty dull stuff to Mr. Bones, but who was he to grumble about his master's enthusiasms? Willy sounded more inspired than at any moment in the past two weeks, and even though his recitation was followed by another brutal coughing fit (more sputum, more gasping, more foot-stomping as he clung to the downspout for dear life), he quickly rebounded once the spasm was over.

"We done hit pay dirt, little pard," Willy said, spitting out the last bits of mucus and pulmonary tissue. "It ain't Miss Bea's house, that's for sure, but give me my druthers, and there's no place on earth I'd rather be than here. This Poe fella was my grandpa, the great forebear and daddy of all us Yankee scribes. Without him, there wouldn't have been no me, no them, no nobody. We've wound up in Poe-land, and if you say it quick enough, that's the same country my own dead ma was born in. An angel's led us to this spot, and I aim to sit here awhile and pay my respects.

Seein' as how I can't take another step anyway, I'd be much obliged if you joined me, Mr. Bones. That's right, take a seat beside me while I rest my pins. Never mind the rain. It's just a few drops is all, and it don't mean us no harm."

Willy let out a long, laboring grunt and then eased himself to the ground. It was a painful thing for Mr. Bones to observe – all that effort to travel just a few inches – and the dog's heart welled up with pity to see his master in such a sorrowful state. He could never be certain exactly how he knew it, but as he watched Willy lower himself to the sidewalk and lean his back against the wall, he knew that he would never get up again. This was the end of their life together. The last moments were upon them, and there was nothing to do now but sit there until the light faded from Willy's eyes.

Still, the trip hadn't worked out so badly. They'd come here looking for one thing and had found another, and in the end Mr. Bones much preferred the thing they'd found to the thing they hadn't. They weren't in Baltimore, they were in Poland. By some miracle of luck or fate or divine justice, Willy had managed to get himself home again. He had returned to the place of his ancestors, and now he could die in peace.

Mr. Bones raised his left hind paw and began

working on an itch behind his ear. In the distance, he saw a man and a little girl walking slowly in the opposite direction, but he didn't trouble himself about them. They would come, they would go, and it made no difference who they were. The rain was coming down harder now, and a small breeze was beginning to kick around the candy wrappers and paper bags in the street. He sniffed the air once, twice, then yawned for no particular reason. After a moment, he curled up on the ground beside Willy, exhaled deeply, and waited for whatever was going to happen next.

2

Nothing did. For the longest time, it was as if the entire neighborhood had stopped breathing. No one walked by, no cars passed, not a single person went in or out of a house. The rain poured down, just as Mr. Bones had predicted it would, but then it slackened, gradually turned into a drizzle again, and at last made a quiet departure from the scene. Willy stirred not a muscle during these skyward agitations. He lay sprawled out against the brick building as before, his eyes shut and his mouth partly open, and if not for the rusty, creaking noise that intermittently emerged from his lungs, Mr. Bones might well have assumed that his master had already slipped into the next world.

That was where people went after they died. Once your soul had been separated from your body, your body was buried in the ground and your soul lit out for the next world. Willy had been harping on this subject for the past several weeks, and by now there was no doubt in the dog's mind that the next world was a real place. It was called Timbuktu, and from everything Mr. Bones could gather, it was located in the middle of a desert somewhere, far from New York or Baltimore, far from Poland or any other city they had visited in the course of their travels. At one point, Willy described it as "an oasis of spirits." At another point he said: "Where the map of this world ends, that's where the map of Timbuktu begins." In order to get there, you apparently had to walk across an immense kingdom of sand and heat, a realm of eternal nothingness. It struck Mr. Bones as a most difficult and unpleasant journey, but Willy assured him that it wasn't, that it took no more than a blink of an eye to cover the whole distance. And once you were there, he said, once you had crossed the boundaries of that refuge, you no longer had to worry about eating food or sleeping at night or emptying your bladder. You were at one with the universe, a speck of anti-matter lodged in the brain of God. Mr. Bones had trouble imagining what life would be like in such a place, but Willy talked about it with such longing, with such pangs of tenderness reverberating in his voice, that the dog eventually gave up his qualms. *Tim–buk–tu*. By now, even the sound of the word was enough to make him happy. The blunt combination of vowels and consonants rarely failed to stir him in the deepest parts of his soul, and whenever those three syllables came rolling off his master's tongue, a wave of blissful well-being would wash through the entire length of his body – as if the word alone were a promise, a guarantee of better days ahead.

It didn't matter how hot it was there. It didn't matter that there was nothing to eat or drink or smell. If that's where Willy was going, that's where he wanted to go too. When the moment came for him to part company with this world, it seemed only right that he should be allowed to dwell in the hereafter with the same person he had loved in the here-before. Wild beasts no doubt had their own Timbuktu, giant forests in which they were free to roam without threat from two-legged hunters and trappers, but lions and tigers were different from dogs, and it made no sense to throw the tamed and untamed together in the afterlife. The strong would devour the weak, and in no time flat every dog in the place would be dead, dispatched to yet another after-life, a beyond beyond the beyond, and what would be the point of arranging things like that? If there was any justice in the world, if the dog god had any influence on what happened to his creatures, then man's best friend would stay by the side of man after said man and said best friend had both kicked the bucket. More than that, in Timbuktu dogs would be able to speak man's language and converse with him as an equal. That was what logic dictated, but who knew if justice or logic had any more impact on the next world than they did on this one? Willy had somehow forgotten to mention the matter, and because Mr. Bones's name had not come up once, *not once* in all their conversations about Timbuktu, the dog was still in the dark as to where he was headed after his own demise. What if Timbuktu turned out to be one of those places with fancy carpets and expensive antiques? What if no pets were allowed? It didn't seem possible, and yet Mr. Bones had lived long enough to know that anything was possible, that impossible things happened all the time. Perhaps this was one of them, and in that *perhaps* hung a thousand dreads and agonies, an unthinkable horror that gripped him every time he thought about it.

Then, against all odds, just as he was about to fall into another one of his funks, the sky began to brighten. Not only had the rain stopped, but the bulked-up clouds overhead were slowly breaking apart, and whereas just an hour before everything had been gray and gloom, now the sky was tinged with color, a motley jumble of pink and yellow streaks that bore down from the west and steadily advanced across the breadth of the city.

Mr. Bones lifted his head. A moment later, as if the two actions were secretly connected, a shaft of light came slanting through the clouds. It struck the sidewalk an inch or two from the dog's left paw, and then, almost immediately, another beam landed just to his right. A crisscross of light and shadow began to form on the pavement in front of him, and it was a beautiful thing to behold, he felt, a small, unexpected gift on the heels of so much sadness and pain. He looked back at Willy then, and just as he was turning his head, a great bucketful of light poured down on the poet's face, and so intense was the light as it crashed against the sleeping man's eyelids that his eyes involuntarily opened – and there was Willy, all but defunct a moment ago, back in the land of the living, dusting off the cobwebs and trying to wake up.

He coughed once, then again, and then a third time before lapsing into a prolonged seizure. Mr. Bones stood by helplessly as globules of phlegm came flying from his master's mouth. Some landed on Willy's shirt, others on the pavement. Still others, the looser and more slithery ones, dribbled weakly down his chin. There they remained, dangling from his beard like noodles, and as the fit wore on, punctuated by violent jolts, lurches, and doublings over, they bobbed back and forth in a crazy, syncopated dance. Mr. Bones was stunned by the ferocity of the attack. Surely this was the end, he said to himself, surely this was the limit of what a man could take. But Willy still had some fight left in him, and once he wiped his face with the sleeve of his jacket and managed to recover his breath, he surprised Mr. Bones by breaking into a broad, almost beatific smile. With much difficulty, he maneuvered himself into a more comfortable position, leaning his back against the wall of the house and stretching out his legs before him. Once his master was still again, Mr. Bones lowered his head on to his right thigh. When Willy reached out and started stroking the top of that head, a measure of calm returned to the dog's broken heart. It was only temporary, of course, and only an illusion, but that didn't mean it wasn't good medicine.

"Lend an ear, Citizen Mutt," Willy said. "It's starting. Things are falling away now. One by one they're falling away, and only strange things are left, tiny long-ago things, not at all the things I was expecting. I can't say I'm scared, though. A little sorry, maybe, a little miffed at having to make this early exit, but not crapping my drawers the way I thought I might be. Pack up your bags, amigo. We're on the road to Splitsville, and there's no turning back. You follow, Mr. Bones? Are you with me so far?"

Mr. Bones followed, and Mr. Bones was with him.

"I wish I could boil it down to a few choice words for you," the dying man continued, "but I can't. Punchy epigrams, succinct pearls of wisdom, Polonius delivering his parting shots. I don't have it in me to do that. Neither a borrower nor a lender be; a stitch in time saves nine. There's too much mayhem in the attic, Bonesy, and you'll just have to bear with me as I ramble and digress. It seems to be in the nature of things for me to be confused. Even now, as I enter the valley of the shadow of death, my thoughts bog down in the gunk of yore. There's the rub, signore. All this clutter in my head, this dust and bric-a-brac, these useless knickknacks spilling off the shelves. Indeed, sir, the sad truth is that I am a bear of but little brain.

"By way of proof, I offer you the return of O'Dell's Hair Trainer. The stuff disappeared from my life forty years ago, and now, on the last day of my life, it suddenly comes back. I yearn for profundities, and what I get is this no-account factoid, this microblip on the screen of memory. My mother used to rub it into my hair when I was just a wee thing, a mere mite of a lad. They sold it in the local barber shops, and it came in a clear glass bottle about yea big. The spout was black, I believe, and on the label there was a picture of some grinning idiot boy. A wholesome, idealized numskull with perfectly groomed hair. No cowlicks for that lunkhead, no wobbles in the part for that pretty fellow. I was five, six years old, and every morning my mother would give me the treatment, hoping to make me look like his twin brother. I can still hear the gloppity-gluggity sound as the goo came out of the bottle. It was a whitish, translucent liquid, sticky to the touch. A kind of watered-down sperm, I suppose, but who know about such things then? They probably manufactured it by hiring teenage boys to jerk off into vats. Thus are fortunes made in our great land. A penny to produce, a dollar to buy, and you figure out the rest. So my Polish mother would rub the O'Dell's Hair Trainer into my scalp, comb my disobedient locks, and then send me off to school looking like that ass-wipe kid on the bottle. I was going to be an American, by gum, and this hair meant that I belonged, that my parents knew what was fucking what.

"Before you break down and weep, my friend, let me add that O'Dell's was a sham concoction, a fraud. It didn't train hair so much as glue it into submission. For the first hour, it would seem to do its job, but then, as the morning wore on, the glue would harden, and little by little my hair would be turned into a mass of rigid, epoxified wires – as if a springy metallic bonnet had been clamped over my head. It felt so strange to the touch, I couldn't leave it alone. Even as my right hand gripped the pencil, making with the two plus threes and six minus fives, my left hand would be wandering around up north, poking and picking at the alien surfaces of my head. By mid-afternoon, the O'Dell's would be so dried out, so thoroughly drained of moisture, that each strand of coated hair would be turned into a brittle thread. That was the moment I was waiting for, the signal that the last act of the farce was about to begin. One by one, I'd reach down to the base of each strand of hair rooted in my scalp, pinch it between my thumb and middle finger, and pull. Slowly. Very slowly, sliding my nails along the entire length of the hair. Ah. The satisfactions were immense, incalculable. All that powder flying off of me! The storms, the blizzards, the whirlwinds of whiteness! It was no easy job, let me tell you, but little by little every trace of the O'Dell's would disappear. The do would be undone, and by the time the last bell rang and the teacher sent us home, my scalp would be tingling with happiness. It was as good as sex, *mon vieux*, as good as all the drugs and drink I ever poured into my system. Five years old, and every day another orgy of self-repair. No wonder I didn't pay attention at school. I was too busy feeling myself up, too busy doing the O'Dell's diddle.

"But enough. Enough of this tedium. Enough of this Te Deum. Hair trainer is just the tip of the iceberg, and once I start in with this childhood drek, we'll be here for the next sixteen hours. We don't have time for that, do we? Not for castor oil, not for pot cheese, not for lumpy porridge, not for Blackjack gum. We all grew up with that junk, but now it's gone, isn't it, and who the hell cares anyway? Wallpaper, that's what it was. Background music. Zeitgeist dust on the furniture of the mind. I can bring back fifty-one thousand details, but so what? It won't do you or me an ounce of good. Understanding. That's what I'm after, chum. The key to the puzzle, the secret formula after four-plus decades of groping in the dark. And still, all this stuff keeps getting in my way. Even as I breathe my last, I'm choking on it. Useless bits of knowledge, unwanted memories, dandelion fluff. It's all flit and fume, my boy, a bellyful of wind. The life and times of R. Mutt. Eleanor Rigby. Rumpelstiltskin. Who the fuck wants to know them? The Pep Boys, the Ritz

Brothers, Rory Calhoun. Captain Video and the Four Tops. The Andrews Sisters, *Life* and *Look*, the Bobbsey Twins. There's no end to it, is there? Henry James and Jesse James, Frank James and William James. James Joyce. Joyce Cary. Cary Grant. Grant me swizzle sticks and dental floss, Dentyne gum and honey-dip doughnuts. Delete Dana Andrews and Dixie Dugan, then throw in Damon Runyon and demon rum for good measure. Forget Pall Malls and shopping malls, Milton Berle and Burl Ives, Ivory soap and Aunt Jemima pancake mix. I don't need them, do I? Not where I'm going I don't, and yet there they are, marching through my brain like long-lost brethren. That's American know-how for you. It keeps coming at you, and every minute there's new junk to push out the old junk. You'd think we would have caught on by now, wised up to the tricks they pull on us, but people can't get enough of it. They cheer, they wave flags, they hire marching bands. Yes, yes, wondrous things, miraculous things, machines to stagger the imagination, but let us not forget, no let us not forget that we are not alone in this world. Know-how knows no borders, and when you think of the bounty that pours in from across the seas, it knocks you down a peg or two and puts you in your place. I don't just mean obvious things like turkeys from Turkey or chili from Chile. I also mean pants from France. I mean pain from Spain and pity from Italy and checks from Czechoslovakia and fleece from Greece. Patriotism has its role, but in the long run it's a sentiment best kept under wraps. Yes, we Yanks have given the world the zipper and the Zippo, not to speak of zip-a-dee-doo-dah and Zeppo Marx, but we're also responsible for the H-bomb and the hula hoop. It all balances out in the end, doesn't it? Just when you think you're top gun, you wind up as bottom dog. And I don't mean you, Mr. Bones. Dog as metaphor, if you catch my drift, dog as emblem of the downtrodden, and you're no trope, my boy, you're as real as they come.

"But don't get me wrong. There's too much out there not to feel tempted. The lure of particulars, I mean, the seductions of the thing-in-itself. You'd have to be blind not to give in once in a while. I don't care what it is. Just pick a thing, and chances are a case can be made for it. The splendor of bicycle wheels, for example. Their lightness, their spidery elegance, their shining rims and gossamer spokes. Or the sound of a manhole cover rattling under a truck at three in the morning. To say nothing of Spandex, which has probably done more to spruce up the landscape than any invention since the underground telephone wire. I refer to the sight of Spandex pants plastered across the behind of a young chick as she strides by you on the street. Need I say more? You'd have to be dead not to warm to that. It darts and dives at you, keeps churning away in your head until it all melts down into a big buttery ooze. Vasco da Gama in his puffy pantaloons. FDR's cigarette holder. Voltaire's powdery wig. Cunégonde! Cunégonde! Think of what happens when you say it. See what you say when you think it. Cartography. Pornography. Stenography. Stentorian stammerings, Episcopalian floozies, Fudgicles and Frosted Flakes. I admit that I've succumbed to the charms of these things as readily as the next man, am in no wise superior to the riffraff I've rubbed shoulders with for lo these many years. I'm human, aren't I? If that makes me a hypocrite, then so be it.

"Sometimes, you just have to bow down in awe. A person comes up with an idea that no one has ever thought of, an idea so simple and perfect that you wonder how the world ever managed to survive without it. The suitcase with wheels, for example. How could it have taken us so long? For thirty thousand years, we've been lugging our burdens around with us, sweating and straining as we moved from one place to another, and the only thing that's ever come of it is sore muscles, bad backs, exhaustion. I mean, it's not as though we didn't have the wheel, is it? That's what gets me. Why did we have to wait until the end of the twentieth century for this gizmo to see the light of day? If nothing else, you'd think roller skates would have inspired someone to make the connection, to put two and two together. But no. Fifty years go by, seventy-five years go by, and people are still schlepping their bags through airports and train stations every time they leave home to visit Aunt Rita in Poughkeepsie. I'm telling you, friend, things aren't as simple as they look. The human spirit is a dull instrument, and often we're no better at figuring out how to take care of ourselves than the lowest worm in the ground.

"Whatever else I've been, I've never let myself be that worm. I've jumped, I've galloped, I've soared, and no matter how many times I've crashed back to earth, I've always picked myself up and tried again. Even now, as the darkness closes in on me, my mind holds fast and won't throw in the towel. The transparent toaster, comrade. It came to me in a vision two or three nights ago, and my head's been full of the idea ever since. Why not expose the works, I said to myself, be able to watch the bread turn from white to golden brown, to see the metamorphosis with your own eyes? What good does it do to lock up the bread and hide it behind that ugly stainless steel? I'm talking about clear glass, with the orange coils glowing within. It would be a thing of beauty, a work of art in every kitchen, a luminous sculpture to contemplate even as we go about the humble task of preparing breakfast and fortifying ourselves for the day ahead. Clear, heat-resistant glass. We could tint it blue, tint it green, tint it any color we like, and then, with the orange radiating from within, imagine the combinations, just think of the visual wonders that would be possible. Making toast would be turned into a religious act, an emanation of other-worldliness, a form of prayer. Jesus god. How I wish I had the strength to work on it now, to sit down and draw up some plans, to perfect the thing and see where we got with it. That's all I've ever dreamed of, Mr. Bones. To make the world a better place. To bring some beauty to the drab, humdrum corners of the soul. You can do it with a toaster, you can do it with a poem, you can do it by reaching out your hand to a stranger. It doesn't matter what form it takes. To leave the world a little better than you found it. That's the best a man can ever do.

"OK, snicker if you like. If I gush, I gush, and that's all there is to it. It feels good to let the purple

73

stuff come pouring out sometimes. Does that make me a fool? Perhaps it does. But better that than bitterness, I say, better to follow the lessons of Santa Claus than to spend your life in the claws of deceit. Sure, I know what you're thinking. You don't have to say it. I can hear the words in your head, *mein Herr*, and you won't get an argument from me. Wherefore this floundering? you ask yourself. Wherefore this flopping to and fro, this rolling in the dust, this lifelong grovel toward annihilation? You do well to ask these questions. I've asked them many times myself, and the only answer I've ever come up with is the one that answers nothing. Because I wanted it this way. Because I had no choice. Because there are no answers to questions like these.

"No apologies, then. I've always been a flawed creature, Mr. Bones, a man riddled with contradictions and inconsistencies, the tugs of too many impulses. On the one hand, purity of heart, goodness, Santa's loyal helper. On the other hand, a loud-mouthed crank, a nihilist, a besotted clown. And the poet? He fell somewhere in between, I suppose, in the interval between the best and the worst of me. Not the saint, and not the wise-cracking drunk. The man with the voices in his head, the one who sometimes managed to listen in on the conversations of stones and trees, who every now and then could turn the music of the clouds into words. Pity I couldn't have been him more. But I've never been to Italy, alas, the place where pity is produced, and if you can't afford the fare, then you just have to stay at home.

"Still, you've never seen me at my best, Sir Osso, and I regret that. I regret that you've known me only as a man in decline. It was a different story back in the old days, before my spunk petered out and I ran into this . . . this engine trouble. I never wanted to be a bum. That wasn't what I had in mind for myself, that wasn't how I dreamed of my future. Scrounging for empty bottles in recycling bins wasn't part of the plan. Squirting water on windshields wasn't part of the plan. Falling down on my knees in front of churches and closing my eyes to look like an early Christian martyr so that some passerby would feel sorry for me and drop a dime or quarter in my palm – no, Signor Puccini, no, no, no, that wasn't what I was put on this earth to do. But man does not live by words alone. He needs bread, and not just one loaf, but two. One for the pocket and one for the mouth. Bread to buy bread, if you see what I mean, and if you don't have the first kind, you sure as hell aren't going to have the other.

"It was a tough blow when *Mom-san* left us. I'm not going to deny that, pupster, and I'm not going to deny that I made things worse by giving away all that money. I said no apologies, but now I want to take that back and apologize to you. I did a rash and stupid thing, and we've both paid the price. Ten thousand dollars ain't Shredded Wheat, after all. I let it slip through my fingers, watched the whole wad scatter to the winds, and the funny thing about it was that I didn't care. It made me happy to act like a big shot, to flaunt my haul like some cockamamie high-roller. Mr. Altruism. Mr. Al Truism, that's me, the one and only Alberto Verissimo, the man who took his mother's life-insurance policy and unloaded every nickel of it. A hundred dollars to Benny Shapiro. Eight hundred dollars to Daisy Brackett. Four thousand dollars to the Fresh Air Fund. Two thousand dollars to the Henry Street Settlement House. Fifteen hundred dollars to the Poets-in-the-Schools Program. It went fast, didn't it? A week, ten days, and by the time I looked up again, I had divested myself of my entire inheritance. Oh well. Easy come easy go, as the old saw says, and who am I to think I could have done otherwise? It's in my blood to be bold, to do the thing that no one else would do. Buck the buck, that's what I did. It was my one chance to put up or shut up, to prove to myself that I meant what I'd been saying for all those years, and so when the dough came in I didn't hesitate. I bucked the buck. I might have fucked myself in the process, but that doesn't mean I acted in vain. Pride counts for something, after all, and when push came to shove, I'm glad I didn't back down. I walked the plank. I went the whole distance. I jumped. Never mind the sea monsters below. I know who I am, as the good sailor Popeye never said, and for once in my life I knew exactly what I was doing.

"Too bad you had to suffer, of course. Too bad we had to hit bottom. Too bad we lost our winter hideout and had to fend for ourselves in ways we weren't accustomed to. It took its toll, didn't it? The bad grub, the lack of shelter, the hard knocks. It turned me into a sick man, and it's about to turn you into an orphan. Sorry, Mr. Bones. I've done my best, but sometimes a man's best isn't good enough. If I could just get back on my feet for a few more minutes, I might be able to figure something out. Settle you in somewhere, take care of business. But my oomph is on the wane. I can feel it dribbling out of me, and one by one things are falling away. Bear with me, dog. I'll rebound yet. Once the discombobulation passes, I'll give it the old college try again. If it passes.

And if it doesn't, then I'm the one who will pass, n'est-ce pas? I just need a little more time. A few more minutes to catch my breath. Then we'll see. Or not see. And if we don't, then there'll be nothing but darkness. Darkness everywhere, as far as the eye can't see. Even down to the sea, to the briny depths of nothingness, where no things are nor will ever be. Except me. Except not me. Except eternity."

Willy stopped talking then, and the hand that had been rubbing the top of Mr. Bones's head for the past twenty-five minutes gradually went limp, then ceased moving altogether. For the life of him, Mr. Bones assumed that this was the end. How not to think that after the finality of the words just spoken? How not to think his master was gone when the hand that had been massaging his skull suddenly slid off him and fell lifelessly to the ground? Mr. Bones didn't dare look up. He kept his head planted on Willy's right thigh and waited, hoping against hope that he was wrong. For the fact was that the air was less still than it should have been. There were sounds coming from somewhere, and as he fought through the miasma of his mounting grief to listen more carefully, he understood that they were coming from his master. Was it possible? Not quite willing to believe his ears, the dog checked again, girding himself against disappointment even as his certainty grew. Yes, Willy was breathing. The air was still going in and out of his lungs, still going in and out of his mouth, still lumbering through the old dance of inhales and exhales, and though the breath was shallower than it had been just a day or two ago, no more than a faint fluttering now, a feathery sibilance confined to the throat and upper lungs, it was nevertheless breath, and where there was breath, there was life. His master wasn't dead. He had fallen asleep.

Not two seconds after that, as if to confirm the accuracy of Mr. Bones's observation, Willy began to snore.

The dog was a nervous wreck by then. His heart had jumped through a hundred hoops of dread and despair, and when he understood that a reprieve had been granted, that the hour of reckoning had been pushed back a little longer, he nearly collapsed with exhaustion. It was all too much for him. When he saw his master sit down on the ground and lean his back against the walls of Poland, he had vowed to stay awake, to keep watch over him until the bitter end. That was his duty, his fundamental responsibility as a dog. Now, as he listened to the familiar dirge of Willy's snoring, he couldn't resist the temptation to close his eyes. The tranquilizing effects of the sound were that powerful. Every night for seven years, Mr. Bones had drifted off to sleep on the waves of that music, and by now it was a signal that all was right with the world, that no matter how hungry or miserable you felt at that moment, the time had come to put aside your cares and float into the land of dreams. After some minor readjustments of position, that was precisely what Mr. Bones did. He laid his head on Willy's stomach, Willy's arm involuntarily lifted itself up into the air, then came down to rest across the dog's back, and the dog fell asleep.

That was when he dreamed the dream in which he saw Willy die. It began with the two of them waking up, opening their eyes and emerging from the sleep they had just fallen into – which was the sleep they were in now, the same one in which Mr. Bones was dreaming the dream. Willy's condition was no worse than it had been before the nap. If anything, it appeared to be a tad better because of it. For the first time in several moons, he didn't cough when he stirred, didn't lapse into another fit, didn't seize up in a gruesome frenzy of gasping, choking, and blood-tinged expectorations. He simply cleared his throat and started talking again, picking up almost exactly where he had left off earlier.

He went on for what seemed to be another thirty or forty minutes, charging ahead in a delirium of half-formed sentences and broken-off thoughts. He swam up from the bottom of the sea, took a deep breath, and began to talk about his mother. He made a list of *Mom-san*'s virtues, countered with a list of her faults, and then begged forgiveness for any sufferings he might have caused her. Before moving on to the next thing, he recalled her talent for bungling jokes, fondly regaling Mr. Bones with examples of her unerring knack for forgetting punch lines at the last minute. Then he reeled off another list – this one of all the women he had ever slept with (physical descriptions included) – and followed that with a long-winded diatribe against the perils of consumerism. Then, suddenly, he was delivering a treatise on the moral advantages of homelessness, which ended with a heartfelt apology to Mr. Bones for dragging him down to Baltimore on what had turned out to be a wild-goose chase. "I forgot to add the letter *g*," he said. "I didn't come for Bea Swanson; I came to give my swan song," and immediately after that he was reciting a new poem, an apostrophe to the invisible demiurge who was about to claim his soul. Apparently composed off the top of his head, its opening stanza went something like this:

O Lord of the ten thousand blast furnaces and
   dungeons,
Of the pulverizing hammer and chain-mail gaze,
Dark Lord of the salt mines and pyramids,
Maestro of the sand dunes and flying fish,
Listen to the prattle of your poor servant,
Dying on the shores of Baltimore
And headed for the Great Beyond . . .

After the poem dribbled away, it was replaced by
more laments and fugues, more unpredictable
sputterings on any number of themes: the Symphony of Smells and why the experiment failed,
Happy Felton and the Knothole Gang (who the
hell was he?), and the fact that the Japanese ate
more rice grown in America than in Japan. From
there he drifted into the ups and downs of his literary career, wallowing for several minutes in a
bog of pent-up grievances and morbid self-pity,
then roused his spirits for a while to talk about
his college roommate (the same one who had
taken him to the hospital in 1968) – a guy named
Anster, Omster, something like that – who had
gone on to write a number of so-so books and
had once promised Willy to find a publisher for
his poems, but of course Willy had never sent
him the manuscript and that was that, but it
proved that he *could* have been published if he'd
wanted to be – he just didn't want to, that's all,

and who the fuck cared about that vainglorious bullshit anyway? The doing was what mattered, not what you did with it after it was done, and as far as he was concerned now, not even the note-books in the Greyhound locker were worth more than a fart and a used-up can of beans. Let them burn, for all he cared, let them be thrown out with the trash, let them be tossed into the men's room for weary travelers to wipe their asses with. He never should have lugged them down to Bal-timore in the first place. A moment of weakness, that's what it was, a last-gasp move in the vile game of Ego – which was the one game that everyone loses, that no one can ever win. He paused for a few moments after that, marveling at the depth of his own bitterness, and then let out a long wheezy laugh, bravely mocking him-self and the world he loved so much. From there he returned to Omster, launching into a story his friend had told him many years before about meeting an English setter in Italy who could write out sentences on a typewriter that had been custom-built for dogs. Inexplicably, Willy broke down in sobs after that, and then he began to berate himself for never having taught Mr. Bones how to read. How could he have neglected to take care of such an essential matter? Now that the dog was about to be cast out on his own, he would need every advantage he could get, and Willy had let him down, had done nothing to provide him with a new situation, was leaving him with no money, no food, no means to cope with the dangers that lay ahead. The bard's tongue was going a mile a minute by then, but Mr. Bones didn't miss a trick, and he could hear Willy's words as distinctly as he had ever heard them in life. That was what was so strange about the dream. There was no distortion, no wavy interference, no sudden switching of channels. It was just like life, and even though he was asleep, even though he was hearing the words in a dream, he was awake in the dream, and therefore the longer he went on sleeping, the more awake he felt.

Midway through Willy's speculations on canine reading skills, a police car pulled up in front of Poe's house, and two large men in uniforms climbed out. One was white and the other was black, and they were both sweating in the August heat, a pair of wide-hipped cops out on Sunday patrol, carrying the instruments of the law around their waists: revolvers and handcuffs, billy clubs and holsters, flashlights and bullets. There was no time to make a full inventory, for no sooner did the men get out of the car than one of them started talking to Willy ("Can't

stay there, pal. You going to move on or what?"),
and at that moment Willy turned, looked straight
into his friend's eyes, and said, "Beat it, Bonesy.
Don't let them catch you," and because Mr.
Bones knew that this was it, that the dreaded
moment was suddenly upon them, he licked
Willy's face, whimpered a brief farewell as his
master patted his head for the last time, and then
took off, charging down North Amity Street as
fast as his legs could take him.

He heard the alarmed voice of one of the cops
shouting behind him ("Frank, get the dog! Get
the fucking dog, Frank!"), but he didn't stop
until he reached the corner, a good eighty or
ninety feet from the house. By then, Frank had
already given up the idea of chasing after him.
As Mr. Bones turned around to see what was
happening to Willy, he saw the white cop wad-
dling back toward the house. A moment later,
urged on by the other one, who was kneeling
over Willy and gesturing wildly with his hands,
Frank broke into a slow trot and went to join his
partner. No one was worried about the dog anymore. There was a dying man to attend to, and as
long as Mr. Bones kept himself at a safe distance,
nothing was going to happen to him.

So he stood on the corner and watched, panting heavily after his short run, the wind all but

knocked out of him. He felt sorely tempted to open his mouth and howl, to let go with one of his dark, bloodcurdling moon wails, but he suppressed the urge, knowing full well that this was no time to vent his sorrows. In the distance, he saw the black cop standing by the car, talking into the two-way radio. A muffled, static-charged response filled the empty street. The cop talked again, and gusts of incomprehensible words followed, another onslaught of noise and gibberish. A door opened across the street, and someone came out to see what was going on. A woman in a yellow house frock and a head full of pink curlers. Two children emerged from another house. A boy of about nine and a girl of about six, both of them wearing shorts and no shoes. Meanwhile, Willy was invisible, still lying where Mr. Bones had left him, blocked off from view by the white cop's broad, hulking body. A minute or two went by, then another minute or two, and then, faintly in the distance, Mr. Bones heard the sound of an approaching siren. By the time the white ambulance turned down North Amity Street and stopped in front of the house, a crowd of a dozen people had gathered, standing around with their hands in their pockets or their arms folded across their chests. Two paramedics jumped out of the back of the ambulance, wheeled a stretcher toward the house, and returned a moment later with Willy on board. It was hard to see much of anything, hard to know whether his master was alive or not. Mr. Bones considered rushing back for a last look, but he hesitated to take such a risk, and by the time he'd made up his mind to do it, the paramedics had already slid Willy into the ambulance and were slamming the doors shut.

Until then, the dream had been no different from reality. Word for word, gesture for gesture, every event had been an exact and faithful rendering of events as they happened in the world. Now, as the ambulance drove off and the people slowly returned to their houses, Mr. Bones felt himself divide in two. Half of him remained on the corner, a dog contemplating his bleak and uncertain future, and the other half of him turned into a fly. Given the nature of dreams, perhaps there was nothing unusual about that. We all change into other things while we sleep, and Mr. Bones was no exception. At one time or another, he had entered the skin of a horse, a cow, and a pig, not to speak of several different dogs, but until he had the dream that day, he had never been two things at once.

There was urgent business to attend to, and only the fly part of him could do it. So, while the dog part of him waited on the corner, the fly rose into the air and flew down the block, chasing after the ambulance as swiftly as his wings could carry him. Because it was a dream, and because the fly could fly faster than any flesh-and-blood fly, it didn't take him long to reach his goal. By the time the ambulance turned the corner on to the next street, he had already attached himself to the back-door handle, and it was in this way that he rode with Willy to the hospital, all six of his feet clamped on to the slightly rusty surface of the handle's leeward side, praying that the wind wouldn't blow him off. It turned out to be a wild jaunt, what with the pothole bumps and the swerves and the sudden stops and starts and the air streaming in on him from all directions, but he managed to hold on, and when the ambulance pulled up to the hospital emergency entrance eight or nine minutes later, his wits were still intact. He hopped off the handle just as one of the paramedics was about to grab hold of it, and then, as the doors were opened and Willy was wheeled out, he hovered a yard or so above the scene, an unobtrusive speck looking down at his master's face. At first, he couldn't tell if Willy was alive or dead, but once the gurney was all the way out and its wheels were on the ground, Mrs. Gurevitch's son opened his eyes. Not much, perhaps, just a crack to let some light in and see what was happening, but even that squint was enough to make the fly's heart skip a beat. "Bea Swanson," Willy mumbled. "Three-sixteen Calvert. Gotta call her. Pronto. Gotta give her the key. Bea's key. Life and death. A matter of."

"Don't worry," one of the paramedics said. "We'll take care of it. But don't talk now. Save your strength, Willy."

Willy. That meant he'd said enough for them to know his name, and if he'd been talking in the ambulance, maybe that meant he wasn't as bad off as he seemed, which in turn meant that maybe with the right medicines and the proper care, he'd pull through after all. Or so mused the fly in Mr. Bones's dream, who was in fact Mr. Bones himself, and because he was a biased witness to the proceedings, we should not begrudge him the consolation of last-minute hopes, even if all traces of hope were gone. But what do flies know? And what do dogs know? And what, for that matter, do men know? It was in God's hands now, and the truth was that there was no turning back.

Nevertheless, in the seventeen hours that remained, a number of extraordinary things happened. The fly saw each one of them, looking down from the ceiling above Bed 34 in the indigents' ward of Our Lady of Sorrows Hospital, and if he hadn't been there on that August day in 1993 to see them with his own eyes, he might not have believed that such things were possible. First of all, Mrs. Swanson was found. Within three hours of Willy's admittance to the hospital, his old teacher came striding down the aisle of the ward, was shown to a chair by Sister Mary Theresa, the staff supervisor of the four PM to midnight shift, and from that moment until Willy left this world, she never once strayed from her student's side. Second of all, after several hours of intravenous feeding and nonstop megadoses of antibiotics and adrenaline, Willy's head seemed to clear somewhat, and he spent the last morning of his life in a state as lucid and serene as any Mr. Bones could remember. Third of all, he died without pain. No convulsions, no upheavals, no cataclysmic fires in his chest. He slipped away slowly, withdrawing from this world by small, imperceptible degrees, and in the end it was as if he were a drop of water evaporating in the sun, shrinking and shrinking until at last he wasn't there anymore.

The fly never actually saw the key change hands. It might have happened at a moment when his attention was briefly diverted, but then again, Willy might have forgotten to mention it.

At the time, it hardly seemed important. Once Bea Swanson entered the room, there were so many other things to think about, so many words to follow and feelings to digest, that he could scarcely remember his own name, let alone Willy's half-cocked scheme for salvaging his literary archive.

Her hair had turned white, and she had put on thirty pounds, but the moment he saw her the fly knew who it was. Physically speaking, there was nothing to set her apart from a million other women her age. Dressed in blue-and-yellow madras shorts, a billowing white blouse, and a pair of leather sandals, she seemed to have stopped thinking about her appearance a long time ago. The plumpness of her arms and legs had grown even more pronounced over the years, and with the dimples in her pudgy knees and the varicose veins bulging from her calves and the flesh sagging from her upper arms, you could easily have mistaken her for a retirement-community golf lady, someone with nothing better to do than roam the back nine in an electric cart and worry about whether she was going to putt out in time for the early-bird special. But this woman's skin was white, not tanned, and instead of sunglasses she had on a pair of no-nonsense wire-rimmed specs. Furthermore, once you looked through the lenses of those drugstore glasses, you discovered eyes of the most remarkable shade of blue. Look into those eyes, and you were trapped. They held you with their warmth and vivacity, their intelligence and watchfulness, the depth of their Scandinavian silences. These were the eyes that Willy had fallen in love with as a boy, and now the fly understood what all the fuss had been about. Forget the short-cropped hair and the chubby legs and the humdrum clothes. Mrs. Swanson was no dowager schoolmarm. She was the goddess of wisdom, and once you fell in love with her, you loved her until the day you died.

Nor was she quite the pushover that Mr. Bones had expected her to be. After listening to Willy go on about Mrs. Swanson's kindness and generosity all the way down to Baltimore, he had imagined her as a soft-hearted sentimentalist, one of those flighty women prone to vast and sudden enthusiasms, who broke down and cried at the smallest provocation and bustled about straightening up after people the moment they stood up from their chairs. The real Mrs. Swanson was anything but. That is to say, the Mrs. Swanson in his dream was anything but. When Mrs. Swanson approached Willy's bed and looked into the face of her former student for the first time in almost thirty years, the fly was startled by the toughness and clarity of her reaction. "Jesus Christ, William," she said, "You've sure made a mess of things, haven't you?"

"I'm afraid so," Willy said. "I'm what you call a world-class fuck-up, the king of the know-nothings."

"At least you knew enough to get in touch with me," Mrs. Swanson said, sitting down in the chair that Sister Mary Theresa had provided for her and taking hold of Willy's hand. "The timing might not be so hot, but better late than never, huh?"

Tears started welling up in Willy's eyes, and for once in his life he was unable to speak.

"It was always touch and go with you, William," Mrs. Swanson continued, "so I can't really say I'm surprised. I'm sure you've done your best. But we're talking about highly combustible materials here, aren't we? You walk around with a load of nitroglycerin in your brain, and sooner or later you're going to bump into something. When it comes right down to it, it's a wonder you didn't blow yourself up a long time ago."

"I walked all the way from New York," Willy answered, apropos of nothing. "Too many miles with too little gas in the tank. It just about did me in. But now that I'm here, I'm glad I came."

"You must be tired."

"I feel like an old sock. But at least I can die happy now."

"Don't talk like that. They're going to fix you up and make you better. You'll see, William. In a couple of weeks, you'll be as good as new."

"Sure. And next year I'm going to run for president."

"You can't do that. You already have a job."

"Not really, I'm sort of unemployed these days. Unemployable, really."

"And what about the Santa Claus business?"

"Oh yeah. That."

"You haven't quit, have you? When you wrote me that letter, it sounded like a lifelong commitment."

"I'm still on the payroll. Been on it for more than twenty years now."

"It must be hard work."

"Yeah, it is. But I'm not complaining. Nobody forced me to do it. I signed up of my own free will, and I've never had any second thoughts. Long hours, though, and not one day off in all that time, but what do you expect? It's not easy doing good works. There's no profit in it. And when there's no money in a thing, people tend to get confused. They think you're up to something, even when you're not."

"Do you still have the tattoo? You mentioned it in a letter, but I've never seen it."

"Sure, it's still there. Take a look if you want."

Mrs. Swanson leaned forward in her chair, lifted the right sleeve of Willy's hospital gown, and there it was. "Very nice," she said. "That's what I'd call a proper Santa Claus."

"Fifty bucks," Willy said. "And worth every penny."

That was how the conversation began. It continued for the whole night and into the next morning, interrupted by occasional visits from the nurses, who came by to replenish Willy's I.V., take his temperature, and empty the bedpan. Sometimes, Willy's strength would flag, and he would suddenly doze off in mid-sentence, sleeping for ten or twenty minutes at a stretch, but he would always come back, rising up from the depths of unconsciousness to join Mrs. Swanson again. If she hadn't been there, the fly realized, it was doubtful that he would have held on as long as he did, but so great was his pleasure at being with her again that he continued to make the effort – for as long as effort was possible. Still, he did not struggle against what was coming, and even after he went through a list of things he had never done in life – never learned to drive a car, never flown in an airplane, never visited a foreign country, never learned to whistle – things he had never done and therefore would never do – it was not so much with regret as a kind of indifference, an attempt to prove to her that none of it mattered. "Dying's no big deal," he said, and by that he meant that he was ready to go, that he was grateful to her for seeing to it that his last hours had not been spent among strangers.

As one might have expected, his last words were about Mr. Bones. Willy had returned to the subject of his dog's future, which he had already mentioned several times before, and was emphasizing to Mrs. Swanson how important it was that she comb the city and find him, that she do everything she could to give him a new home. "I've botched it," he said. "I've let my pooch down." And Mrs. Swanson, who was alarmed to see how weak he had suddenly become, tried to soothe him with a few meaningless words, "Don't worry, William, it's all right, it's not important," and Willy, rousing himself for one last effort, managed to lift his head and say, "Yes it is. It's very important –" and then, just like that, his life stopped.

Sister Margaret, the nurse on duty at that hour, walked over to the bed and checked for a pulse. When none could be found, she took a small mirror out of her pocket and held it up to Willy's mouth. A few moments later, she turned the mirror around and looked into it, but the only thing she saw there was herself. Then she put the mirror back in her pocket, reached out with her right hand, and closed Willy's eyes.

"It was a beautiful death," she said.

For all response, Mrs. Swanson covered her face with her hands and wept.

Mr. Bones looked down at her through the eyes of the fly, listening to her grief-stricken sobs fill the ward, and wondered if there had ever been an odder, more perplexing dream than this one. Then he blinked, and he was no longer in the hospital, no longer the fly, but back on the corner of North Amity Street as his old dog self, watching the ambulance drive away into the distance. The dream was over, but he was still inside the dream, which meant that he had dreamed a dream within the dream, a parenthetical reverie of flies and hospitals and Mrs. Swansons, and now that his master was dead, he was back inside the first dream. That's what he imagined, in any case, but no sooner did this thought occur to him than he blinked a second time and woke up, and there he was again, camped out in Poland with the recumbent Willy, who was just waking up himself, and so befuddled was Mr. Bones for the next little while that he wasn't sure if he was really in the world again or had woken up in another dream.

But that wasn't all. Even after he had sniffed the air, rubbed his nose into Willy's leg, and confirmed that this was his true and authentic life, there were more mysteries to contend with. Willy cleared his throat, and as Mr. Bones waited for the inevitable coughing fit, he remembered that Willy hadn't coughed in the dream, that for once his friend had been spared that agony. Now, unexpectedly, it happened again. His master cleared his throat, and immediately after that he was talking again. At first, Mr. Bones dismissed it as a fortunate coincidence, but as Willy continued to talk, charging impetuously from one corner of his mind to another, the dog could not help but notice the resemblance between the words he was listening to and the words he had just heard in the dream. It wasn't that they were exactly the same – at least he didn't think they were – but they were close enough, *close enough*. One by one, Willy touched on each and every topic that had come up in the dream, and when Mr. Bones realized that it was happening in precisely the same order as before, he felt a chill go down his spine. First *Mom-san* and the bungled jokes. Then the catalogue of sexual adventures. Then the diatribes and the apologies, the poem, the literary battles, the whole bit. When he came to the roommate's story about the dog who could type, Mr. Bones wondered if he were going mad. Had he slipped back into the dream, or was the dream just an earlier version of what was happening now? He blinked his eyes, hoping he would wake up. He blinked them again, and again nothing happened. He couldn't wake up because he was already awake. This was his true and authentic life, and because you got to live that life only once, he knew that they had really come to the end this time. He knew that the words tumbling from his master's mouth were the last words he would ever hear Willy speak.

"I wasn't there myself," the bard was saying, "but I trust my witness. In all the years we were friends, I never knew him to make up stories. That's one of his problems, maybe – as a writer, I mean – not enough imagination – but as a friend he always gave it to you straight from the horse's mouth. A lovely phrase that, though I'll be damned if I know what it means. The only talking horse I ever saw was the one in those movies. Donald O'Connor, the army, three or four asinine flicks I sat through as a kid. Now that I think about it, though, it might have been a mule. A mule in the movies, and a horse on TV. What was the name of that show? *Mr. Ed.* Jesus, there I go again. I can't get rid of this garbage. Mr. Ed, Mr. Moto, Mr. Magoo, they're in there still, every last one of them. Mr. Go-Fuck-Yourself. But I'm talking about dogs, aren't I? Not horses, dogs. And not talking dogs either. Not those dogs in the stories about the guy who goes into the bar and bets his life savings because his dog can talk and nobody believes him, and then the dog never opens its mouth, and when the guy asks him about it afterward, the dog says he just couldn't think of anything to say. No, not the talking dog in those dumb jokes, but the typing dog my friend saw in Italy when he was seventeen years old. That's right, Italy. Nitty-gritty Italy, land of the witty ditty and the itty-bitty titty – yet one more place I've never been to.

"His aunt had moved there some years earlier, reasons unknown, and one summer he went to visit her for a couple of weeks. That's a fact, and what makes the dog business ring true is that the dog wasn't even the point of the story. I was reading a book. *The Magic Mountain* it was, written by one Thomas Mann – not to be confused with Thom McAn, renowned cobbler to the masses. I never finished the damned thing by the way, it was so boring, but said Herr Mann was a muckity-muck, a hotshot in the Writers Hall of Fame, and I figured I should take a look. So there

I was reading this massive tome in the kitchen, hunched over a bowl of Cheerios, and my room-mate Paul walks in, sees the title, and says, 'I never finished that one. Started it four times, and I never got past page two-seventy-four.' 'Well,' I said, 'I'm on page two-seventy-one. I guess that means my time is almost up,' and then he tells me, standing there in the doorway and blowing cigarette smoke out of his mouth, that he once met Thomas Mann's widow. Not bragging about it, just stating a fact. That was how he got into the story about going to Italy to visit his aunt, who turned out to be a friend of one of Mann's daughters. He had a lot of kids, old Tom did, and this girl had wound up marrying some well-heeled Italian chap and lived in a nice house up in the hills somewhere outside of God knows what little town. One day Paul and his aunt were invited to the house for lunch, and the hostess's mother was there – Thomas Mann's widow, an old woman with white hair sitting in a rocker and staring into space. Paul shook her hand, nothing of any importance was said, and then they all sat down to lunch. Blah, blah, blah, please pass the salt. Just when you think it's going nowhere, that this is the end of a truly nothing story, Paul learns that Mann's daughter is something called an animal psychologist. And what, you may ask, is an animal psychologist? Your guess is as good as mine, Mr. Bones. After lunch, she takes Paul upstairs and introduces him to an English setter named Ollie, a dog of no particular intelligence as far as he can see, and shows him a huge manual typewriter, which has to be the largest typewriter in the history of creation. It's fitted out with a set of specially designed keys, big concave cups to accommodate the dog's snout. Then she picks up a box of biscuits, calls Ollie over to the typewriter, and gives Paul a demonstration of what the hound can do.

"It was a slow, arduous business, not at all what you would expect. The sentence he was supposed to type was: 'Ollie is a good dog.' Instead of just saying the words to him – or instead of spelling out the words and waiting for him to hit the right letters – she went through each *sound* of each word, breaking the words down into their component phonemes, and pronouncing them so slowly, with such odd inflections and throaty timbres, that she sounded like a deaf person trying to speak. 'Ohhhhh,' she began, 'ohhhhh,' and when the dog pushed his nose down on the letter *O*, she rewarded him with a biscuit, some lovey-dovey talk, and many pats on the head, and then she went on to the next sound, 'l–l–l–l, l–l–l–l,' speaking as slowly and painstakingly as before, and when the dog got it right, she gave him another biscuit and more pats on the head, and so it went, letter by excruciating letter, until they came to the end of the sentence: 'Ollie is a good dog.'

"My friend told me that story twenty-five years ago, and I still don't know if it proves anything. But I do know this: I've been a dunce. I've wasted too much of our time on idle pleasures and frolics, frittered away the years on japes and follies, dreamy bagatelles, unrelenting fracas. We should have borne down and studied, sir, mastered the ABCs, done something useful with the short time allotted us. My fault. All my fault. I don't know about that Ollie character, but you would have achieved far greater things than that, Mr. Bones. You had the head for it, you had the will, you had the guts. But I didn't think your eyes were up to the task, and so I didn't bother. Laziness, that's what it was. Mental sloth. I should have given it a try, refused to take no for an answer. Only out of stubbornness are great things born. Instead, what did I do? I dragged you out to Uncle Al's novelty shop in Coney Island, that's what I did. Got you on to the F train by pretending to be a blind man, tapping my way down the stairs with that white stick, and there you were at my side, snug in your harness, as good a seeing-eye dog as there ever was, not one notch below those Labs and shepherds they send to school to learn the job. Thank you for that, amigo. Thank you for playing along so nobly, for indulging me in my whims and improvisations. But I should have done better by you. I should have given you a chance to reach the stars. It's possible, believe me it is. I just didn't have the courage of my convictions. But the truth is, friend, that dogs can read. Why else would they put those signs on the doors of post offices? NO DOGS ALLOWED EXCEPT FOR SEEING-EYE DOGS. Do you catch my meaning? The man with the dog can't see, so how can he read the sign? And if he can't read it, who else is left? That's what they do in those seeing-eye schools. They just don't tell us. They've kept it a secret, and by now it's one of the three or four best-kept secrets in America. For good reason, too. If word got out, just think of what would happen. Dogs as smart as men? A blasphemous assertion. There'd be riots in the streets, they'd burn down the White House, mayhem would rule. In three months, dogs would be pressing for their independence. Delegations would convene, negotiations would begin, and in the end they'd settle the thing by giving up Nebraska, South Dakota, and half of Kansas. They'd kick out the human population and let the dogs move in, and from then on the country would be divided in two. The United States of People and the Independent Republic of Dogs. Good Christ, how I'd love to see that. I'd move there and work for you, Mr. Bones. I'd fetch your slippers and light your pipe. I'd get you elected prime minister. Anything you want, boss, and I'd be your man."

With that sentence, Willy's rhapsody came to an abrupt halt. A noise had distracted him, and when he turned his head to see what the disturbance was, he let out a little groan. A police car was inching its way down the street, moving in the direction of the house. Mr. Bones didn't have to look to know what it was, but he looked anyway. The car had pulled up alongside the curb, and the two cops were getting out, patting their holsters and adjusting their belts, the black one and the white one, the same two jokers as before. Mr. Bones turned to Willy then, just as Willy was turning to him, and with the cop's words suddenly wafting in from the street ("Can't stay there, pal. You going to move on or what?"), Willy looked him in the eyes and said, "Beat it, Bonesy. Don't let them catch you." So he licked his master's face, stood stock-still for a moment as Willy patted his head, and then he sprinted off, flying down the street as if there were no tomorrow.

3

He didn't stop at the corner this time, and he didn't stand around and wait for the ambulance to show up. What would have been the point? He knew it was coming, and once it got there, he knew where his master was headed. The nuns and doctors would do what they could, Mrs. Swanson would hold his hand and make small talk into the night, and not long after dawn broke the next morning, Willy would be on his way to Timbuktu.

So Mr. Bones kept running, never questioning that the dream would make good on all of its promises, and by the time he rounded the corner and started down the next block, it had already dawned on him that the world wasn't going to end. He almost felt sorry about it now. He had left his master behind, and the ground had not caved in and swallowed him up. The city had not disappeared. The sky had not burst into flames. Everything was as it had been, as it would continue to be, and what was done was done. The houses were still standing, the wind was still blowing, and his master was going to die. The dream had told him that, and because the dream wasn't a dream but a vision of things to come, there was no room for doubt. Willy's fate was sealed. As Mr. Bones trotted along the sidewalk, listening to a siren approach the area he had just left, he understood that the last part of the story was about to begin. But it wasn't his story anymore, and whatever happened to Willy from this point on would have nothing to do with him. He was on his own, and like it or not, he would have to keep on moving, even if he had nowhere to go.

What a confusion those last hours had been, he said to himself, what a hodgepodge of memories and garbled thoughts – but Willy had hit the nail on the head about one thing, and even though he'd gotten a little carried away at the end, you couldn't argue with the basic idea. If Mr. Bones had known how to read, he wouldn't have been in the mess he was in now. Even with the skimpiest, most rudimentary knowledge of the alphabet, he would have been able to hunt down 316 Calvert Street, and once he got there, he would have waited by the door until Mrs. Swanson showed up. She was the only person he knew in Baltimore, but after spending all those hours with her in the dream, he was convinced that she would have been glad to let him in – and have done a crackerjack job of taking care of him to boot. You could tell that just by looking at her, just by listening to her talk. But how to find an address if you couldn't read the street signs? If Willy thought reading was so important, why hadn't he done something about it? Instead of moaning and groaning about his failures and ineptitudes, he could have saved his tears and given him a few quick lessons. Mr. Bones would have been more than willing to have a go at it. That didn't mean he would have succeeded, but how could you know unless you tried?

He turned down another street and stopped to drink from a puddle that had formed during the recent rain. As his tongue lapped up the warm, grayish water, a new thought suddenly occurred to him. Once he had pondered it for a little while, he became almost sick with regret. Forget reading, he said to himself. Forget the arguments about the intelligence of dogs. The whole problem could have been solved in a single, elegant stroke: by hanging a sign around his neck. *My name is Mr. Bones. Please take me to Bea Swanson's house at 316 Calvert Street.* On the back, Willy could have written a note to Mrs. Swanson, explaining what had happened to him and why she should give his dog a home. Once Mr. Bones had hit the streets, there was an excellent chance that some kind-hearted stranger would have read the sign and carried out the request, and within a matter of hours Mr. Bones would have been curled up peacefully on the rug in the living room of his new owner's house. As he turned from the puddle and moved on, Mr. Bones wondered how this idea could have occurred to him, a mere dog, and never once have crossed Willy's mind, which was capable of such breathtaking somersaults and dazzling pirouettes. Because Willy had no sense of the practical, that's why, and because his brain was in a muddle, and because he was sick and dying and in no shape to know which end was up. At least he had talked to Mrs. Swanson about it – or at least he was going to, once Mrs. Swanson arrived at the hospital. "Comb the city for him," he was going to say, and after giving her a full description of what Mr. Bones looked like, he was going to take hold of her hand and beg her to do the right thing. "He needs a home. If you don't take him in, he's cooked." But Willy wasn't going to die until tomorrow, and by the time Mrs. Swanson left the hospital and went home, Mr. Bones would have been wandering the streets all day, all night, and far into the next day. She might not feel up to looking for him until later, perhaps not even until the day after that, and this Baltimore was a big place, a city with ten thousand streets and alleyways, and who knew where he would be then? In order for them to find each other, they would need luck, immense amounts of luck, luck on the scale of a miracle. And Mr. Bones, who no longer believed in miracles, told himself not to count on it.

There were enough puddles to slake his thirst whenever his throat went dry, but food was another matter, and after not having swallowed a morsel for nearly two days, his stomach was crying out to be filled. So it was that his body gradually won out over his mind, and his peevish brooding over missed opportunities gave way to an all-out search for grub. It was late morning now, perhaps even early afternoon, and people were finally up and about, roused from their Sunday torpors and shuffling around their kitchens preparing breakfast and brunch. From nearly every house he trotted past he was assaulted by the smells of bacon cooking on the stove, eggs frying in the skillet, and warm toast popping out of the toaster. It was a foul trick, he felt, a cruel thing to be doing to him in his present state of angst and semi-starvation, but he resisted the urge to go begging for scraps at the doors and kept on moving. Willy's lessons had sunk in. A stray dog is nobody's friend, and if he made a nuisance of himself in front of the wrong person, he'd be carted off to the pound – the place from which no dog ever returned.

If he had developed the habit of hunting and foraging for himself, he wouldn't have felt so helpless now. But he had spent too many years at Willy's side, knocking around the world in his role as confidant and *chien à tout faire*, and whatever lupine instincts he had been born with had long since atrophied and disappeared. He had grown into a soft, civilized creature, a thinking dog instead of an athletic dog, and as far back as he could remember his bodily needs had been taken care of by someone else. But that was the bargain, wasn't it? The man gave you food and a place to sleep, and in return you gave him love and undying loyalty. Now that Willy was gone, he would have to unlearn everything he knew and start all over again. Were changes of that magnitude possible? Mr. Bones had run into homeless dogs in the past, but he had never felt anything but pity for them – pity, and a touch of disdain. The loneliness of their lives was too brutal to contemplate, and he had always kept himself at a safe distance, wary of the ticks and fleas hidden in their fur, reluctant to get too close to them for fear that the diseases and desperation they carried would rub off on him. Perhaps he had turned into a snob, but he could always recognize one of those abject creatures from a hundred yards away. They moved differently from other dogs, gliding along with that grim mendicant's lope of theirs, the tail cocked between their legs at quarter-mast, cantering down the avenues as if they were late for an appointment somewhere – when in fact they weren't going anywhere, just traveling around in circles, lost in the limbo between one nowhere and the next. Now, as he turned another corner and crossed the street, Mr. Bones discovered that he was moving just like that himself. He had kissed his master good-bye less than half an hour ago, and already he was one of them.

By and by, he came to the edge of a traffic circle with an island in the middle of it. A large statue rose up from the island, and as Mr. Bones studied the work from a distance, he concluded that it was supposed to be a soldier on horseback with his sword drawn, as if about to plunge into battle. More interestingly, a flock of pigeons had alighted on various parts of the soldier's body, not to speak of several places on the huge stone horse, and with several other species of birds in attendance below – wrens, sparrows, whatever you called them – Mr. Bones wondered if this might not be a good moment to test his prowess as a killer. If he couldn't depend on people for his food anymore, what choice did he have but to depend on himself?

The traffic had increased by then, and it took some nimble footwork for Mr. Bones to cross to the other side: dodging cars, pausing, rushing forward, waiting again, timing his moves so as not to get hit. At one point, a man on a motorcycle came roaring past him, a bolt of shining black metal that seemed to have materialized out of thin air, and Mr. Bones had to jump to the side to avoid him, which put him smack in front of an oncoming car, a big yellow job with a grille like a waffle iron, and if Mr. Bones hadn't hopped back to where he'd been a second before (returning to the spot the motorcycle had just vacated), that would have been the end of him. Two or three horns honked, a man stuck his head out of a car window and yelled something that sounded like "funderflew" or "chuck and chew," and Mr. Bones felt the sting of the insult. He was ashamed of himself, humiliated by his sorry performance. He couldn't even get to the other side of the road without running into trouble, and if simple things like that were going to be hard for him, what would happen when he came to things that were really hard? In the end, he got to where he was going, but by the time he was out of danger and stepping on to the curb of the island, he felt so rattled and disgusted with himself, he wished he hadn't attempted the crossing in the first place.

Luckily, the traffic had forced him to take the long way around, and he landed on the north side of the island. From that angle, he found himself looking up at the back of the statue, the part that showed the horse's rump and the spokes of the soldier's spurs, and since most of the pigeons had congregated around in the front, Mr. Bones had a little time to catch his breath and plot his next move. He had never been one to chase after birds, but he had watched how other dogs did it, and he had learned enough from them to have formed a fairly good idea of what not to do. You couldn't just blunder in and hope for the best, for example, and you couldn't make a lot of noise, and you couldn't run, no matter how strong the temptation. You weren't out to scare the pigeons, after all. The object was to get one of them in your mouth, and the moment you started to run, they would take off into the air and fly away. That was another point to remember, he told himself. Pigeons could fly, and dogs couldn't. Pigeons might be stupider than dogs, but that was because God had given them wings instead of brains, and in order to overcome those wings, a dog had to reach down inside himself and call upon every trick that life had taught him.

Stealth was the answer. A sneak attack behind enemy lines. Mr. Bones walked over to the western face of the plinth and peered around the corner. A good eighteen or twenty pigeons were still there, parading back and forth in the sunlight. He went down into a crouch, zeroing in on the nearest bird as his belly touched the ground, and then he began to crawl forward, advancing as slowly and surreptitiously as he could. The instant he came into view, three or four sparrows rose up from the pavement and repositioned themselves on the soldier's head, but the pigeons seemed not to notice him. They continued to go about their business, cooing and strutting around in that featherheaded way of theirs, and as he moved toward his chosen victim, he could see what a fine, plump specimen she was, truly a first-rate catch. He would aim for her neck, pouncing on her from behind with his jaws open, and if he jumped at the right moment, she wouldn't have a chance. It was all a matter of patience, of knowing when to strike. He paused, not wanting to stir up any suspicions, trying to blend into the surroundings, to make himself as still and inanimate as the stone horse. He just needed to get a little closer, narrow the gap by another foot or two before springing into action for the final thrust. He was scarcely breathing by then, scarcely moving a muscle, and yet off to his right, at the outer edge of the flock, half-a-dozen pigeons suddenly flapped their wings and took off into the air, rising up toward the statue like a squadron of helicopters. It hardly seemed possible. He had been doing everything by the book, never once deviating from the plan he had set in motion, and yet they were on to him now, and if he didn't act fast, the whole operation was going to blow up in his face. The little prize in front of him waddled forward with a series of rapid, sure-footed steps, quickly retreating out of range. Another pigeon flew off, and then another, and then one more. All hell was breaking loose, and Mr. Bones, who until then had exercised the strictest, most admirable self-control, could think of nothing better to do than leap to his feet and rush after his victim. It was a desperate, thoughtless move, but it almost worked. He felt a wing flutter against his snout just as his jaws were opening, but that was as close as he got. His meal flew off into the air, escaping along with every other bird on the island, and lo and behold, there was Mr. Bones, suddenly alone, galloping back and forth in a frenzy of frustration, jumping into the air and barking, barking at all of them, barking out of rage and defeat, and long after the last bird had disappeared around the steeple of the church on the other side of the avenue, he went on barking – at himself, at the world, at nothing at all.

Two hours later, he discovered an ice-cream cone melting on the sidewalk near the Maritime Museum (cherry vanilla, with candy sprinkles studded in the soft, sugary blob), and then, not fifteen minutes after that, he chanced upon the remnants of a Kentucky Fried Chicken dinner that someone had left on a public bench – a red-and-white take-out box filled with three partially eaten legs, two untouched wings, a biscuit, and a clump of mashed potatoes soaked in brown, salty gravy. The food helped to restore his confidence somewhat, but far less than one might have supposed. The island debacle had shaken him deeply, and for hours afterward the memory of the botched attack kept knifing its way into his consciousness. He had disgraced himself, and even though he tried not to dwell on what had happened, he couldn't escape the feeling that he was old and washed up, a has-been.

He spent the night in a vacant lot, cowering under a profusion of weedy growths and pin-prick stars, barely able to keep his eyes shut for more than five unbroken minutes. Bad as the day had been, the night was even worse, for this was the first night he had ever spent alone, and Willy's absence was so strong, so palpable in the air around him, that Mr. Bones did little else but lie there on his patch of ground and long for the closeness of his master's body. By the time he finally drifted off into something that resembled true sleep, it was almost morning, and three quarters of an hour later the first rays of the rising sun forced his eyes open again. He stood up and shook himself, and at that moment a terrible heaviness swept through him. It was as if everything had suddenly gone dark, as if an eclipse were taking place inside his soul, and while it was never clear to him exactly how he knew it, he was certain that the moment had come for Willy to leave this world. It was just as the dream had foretold. His master was about to die, and in another minute Sister Margaret would come into the room and put the mirror to his mouth, and then Mrs. Swanson would cover her face with her hands and start to weep.

When the fatal moment arrived, his legs buckled and he dropped to the ground. It was as if the very air had flattened him, and for the next few minutes he lay there among the bottle caps and empty beer cans, unable to move. He felt that his body was about to disintegrate, that his vital fluids were going to spill out of him, and once he had been sucked dry, he would be turned into a stiffening carcass, a lump of former dog rotting in the Maryland sun. Then, as unexpectedly as it had come on, the heaviness began to lift, and he felt his life stirring inside him again. But Mr. Bones longed for annihilation now, and rather than stand up and leave the spot where he had experienced Willy's death, he rolled on to his back and spread his legs wide open – exposing his throat, belly, and genitals to the sky. He was utterly vulnerable to attack in that position. Splayed out in puppylike innocence, he waited for God to strike him dead, fully prepared to offer himself up as a sacrifice now that his master was gone. A few more minutes went by. Mr. Bones closed his eyes, steeling himself for the bright, ecstatic blow from above, but God paid no attention to him – or else could not find him – and little by little, as the sun burned through the clouds overhead, Mr. Bones understood that he was not destined to die that morning. He rolled over and climbed to his feet. Then, tilting his head toward the sky, he filled his lungs with air and let out a long, mighty howl.

By ten o'clock, he had fallen in with a gang of six twelve-year-old boys. At first, it seemed like a stroke of good fortune, and for an hour or two he was given the royal treatment. The boys fed him pretzels, hot dogs, and crusts of pizza, and Mr. Bones returned their generosity by doing what he could to keep them entertained. He had never had much to do with children, but he had seen enough over the years to know that they were unpredictable. These boys struck him as a particularly rowdy and boisterous lot. They were full of taunts and swagger and boastful remarks, and after he had been with them for a while, he noticed that they seemed to take an uncommon delight in punching each other and delivering surreptitious whacks to the head. They wound up in a park, and for an hour or so the boys played football, banging into each other's bodies with such vehemence that Mr. Bones began to grow alarmed that someone would get hurt. It was the end of summer vacation. School would be starting again soon, and the boys were hot and bored, itching to stir up trouble. After the game was over, they wandered to the edge of a pond and began skipping stones across the surface of the water. This rapidly degenerated into a contest over whose stone had made the most skips, which in turn led to several heated arguments. Mr. Bones, who despised conflict in any form, decided to break the increasingly rancorous atmosphere by diving into the water and fetching one of the stones. He had never been very interested in retrieving objects. Willy had always shunned that sport as something unworthy of Mr. Bones's intelligence, but Mr. Bones knew how impressed people were when dogs came romping back to their masters with sticks and balls between their teeth, and so he went against his own inclinations and took the plunge. The splash caused a great commotion in the pond, and even as he dove under the surface and deftly snatched a sinking stone in his jaws, he could hear one of the boys cursing him for making such a disturbance. The game was ruined, the boy shouted, and it would take five minutes before the water was still enough to start again. Maybe so, Mr. Bones said to himself as he paddled back to shore, but think how amazed he'll be when I drop this little sucker at his feet. It's not every dog who can pull off a coup like this. When he arrived in front of the angry boy and let go of the stone, however, he was greeted by a kick in the ribs. "Dumb dog," the boy said. "What do you want to mess up our water for?" Mr. Bones let out a yelp of pain and surprise, and immediately after that another dispute flared up among the boys. Some condemned the kick, others applauded it, and before long two of the boys were rolling around on the ground in each other's arms, re-enacting the age-old struggle of might versus right. Mr. Bones withdrew to a safer distance several yards off, shook the water out of his fur, and then stood there waiting for one of the kinder boys to call him back. For all his willingness to bury the hatchet, no one even looked at him. The fighting continued, and when it was finally over, one of the boys spotted him, picked up a stone, and threw it in his direction. It missed by two or three feet, but Mr. Bones had seen enough by then to get the message. He turned and ran away, and even though one or two of the boys shouted after him to come back, he didn't stop running until he had reached the other end of the park.

He spent the next hour sulking under a clump of hawthorn bushes. It wasn't that the kick had hurt so much, but his morale had been bruised, and he was disappointed in himself for having misread the situation so badly. He would have to learn to be more cautious, he told himself, to be less trusting, to assume the worst in people until they had demonstrated their good intentions. It was a sad lesson to be absorbing so late in life, he realized, but if he meant to cope with the difficulties ahead, he would have to toughen up and get with the program. What he needed was to establish some general principles, firm rules of conduct that he could fall back on in moments of crisis. Based on his recent experience, it wasn't hard to come up with the first item on the list. No more kids. No more people under sixteen, especially boy people. They lacked compassion, and once you stripped that quality from a two-leg's soul, he was no better than a mad dog.

Just as he was about to climb out from under the shrub and move on, he spotted a white sneaker not two feet from his nose. It was so like the sneaker that had just landed in his gut that Mr. Bones nearly gagged on his saliva. Had the scoundrel come back to continue the job? The dog recoiled, retreating farther into the tangle of thorns and low-lying branches, snagging his fur in the process. What a dreary predicament to be in now, he thought, but what alternative did he have? He had to keep himself hidden, flattened down on all fours with a dozen spikes in his back, and hope that the bully would get tired of waiting and leave.

But such luck was not to be granted to Mr. Bones that day. The ruffian held his ground, refusing to give up, and instead of taking his mischief to some other area of the park, he crouched down in front of the bush and parted the branches to look in. Mr. Bones growled, ready to pounce on the thug if he had to.

"Don't be afraid," the boy said. "I'm not going to hurt you."

Like hell you aren't, Mr. Bones thought, and because he was still too afraid to let his guard down, he failed to realize that the gentle voice floating through the branches wasn't a trick – but the voice of an altogether different boy.

"I saw what they did to you," the new boy said. "They're jerks, those guys. I know them from school. Ralph Hernandez and Pete Bondy. You hang around with creeps like them, and something bad is always going to happen to you."

By then, the speaker had poked his head in far enough for Mr. Bones to get a clear view of his features, and at last he understood that he wasn't looking at his tormentor. The face belonged to a Chinese boy of ten or eleven, and in that first indelible instant, Mr. Bones felt that it was one of the loveliest human faces he had ever had the pleasure to gaze upon. So much for general principles and rules of conduct. This kid meant him no harm, and if Mr. Bones was wrong about that, then he would turn in his dog badge and spend the rest of his life as a porcupine.

"My name is Henry," the boy said. "Henry Chow. What's your name?"

Ha, thought Mr. Bones. A little wise guy. And how does he think I'm supposed to answer that one?

Still, with so much riding on the outcome of the conversation, he decided to give it his best shot. Buried among the twigs and dead leaves, he raised his head and emitted a series of three quick barks: wŏof, wŏof, wŏof. It was a perfect anapest, with each syllable of his name accorded the proper stress, balance, and duration. For a few brief seconds, it was as if the words Mis|ter Bones had been boiled down to their sonorous essence, to the purity of a musical phrase.

"Good dog," young Henry said, holding out his right hand as a peace offering. "You catch on fast, don't you?"

Mr. Bones barked once more to convey his agreement, and then he began to lick the open palm of the hand that was dangling in front of him. Little by little, Henry coaxed him out from the safety of his hiding place, and once Mr. Bones had fully emerged, the boy sat down on the ground with him and, in between numerous pats on the head and kisses on the face, carefully picked out the leaves and brambles that had collected in his fur.

Thus began an exemplary friendship between dog and boy. In age, they were only three and a half years apart, but the boy was young and the dog was old, and because of that discrepancy, each wound up giving to the other something he had never had before. For Mr. Bones, Henry proved that love was not a quantifiable substance. There was always more of it somewhere, and even after one love had been lost, it was by no means impossible to find another. For Henry, an only child whose parents worked long hours and had steadfastly refused to allow a pet in the apartment, Mr. Bones was the answer to his prayers.

Nevertheless, this budding alliance was not without its pitfalls and its dangers. Once Henry began to talk about his father, Mr. Bones understood that throwing in his lot with this boy was not quite the sure bet it had seemed at first glance. They were slowly wending their way toward the street where the Chow family lived, and as Henry continued to describe the various problems the two of them would be up against, Mr. Bones found himself advancing from anxiety to fear to outright terror. It was bad enough that Henry's father disliked dogs and that Mr. Bones would be barred from entering the house. Worse still was the fact that even after a place had been found for him, his presence would have to be kept a secret from Mr. Chow. If Henry's father caught so much as a whiff of the dog anywhere in the neighborhood, the boy would be punished so severely that he would wish he had never been born. Given that Mr. Chow both lived and worked in the same building, it seemed almost preposterous for them to think they could avoid discovery. The family apartment was upstairs on the second floor, the family business was downstairs on the first floor, and Henry's father was always around, either sleeping or working, morning, noon, and night.

"I know it doesn't look too good," Henry said. "But I'm willing to give it a try if you are."

Well, at least the boy had spirit. And a pleasant voice to go along with it, Mr. Bones added, doing everything he could to look on the bright side and count his blessings. What he didn't know at that point, however, was that the worst was still to come. He had heard the bad, he had heard the worse, but it wasn't until Henry started talking about hiding places that he understood the full horror of what he was getting himself into.

There was the alley, Henry said. That was one option, and if Mr. Bones was willing to sleep in a cardboard box and promised not to make any noise, they might get away with it. Another possibility was the yard around in the back. It wasn't very big – just a patch of weeds, really – with some rusting refrigerators and corroded metal shelves lined up along the fence, but the waiters sometimes went out there to smoke, and on most evenings, especially when the weather was warm, his father liked to spend a few minutes walking around back there after he locked up the restaurant for the night. He called it "drinking in the stars," and according to Henry, he always slept better if he had his little dose of sky before going upstairs and climbing into bed.

Henry rattled on for a while about his father's sleeping habits, but Mr. Bones was no longer listening. The fatal word had passed the boy's lips, and once Mr. Bones realized that the *restaurant* in question was not just any two-bit hot-dog stand but a *Chinese restaurant*, he was ready to turn tail and run. How many times had Willy warned him about those places? Just yesterday morning, he had lectured him for fifteen minutes on the subject, and was Mr. Bones going to ignore that advice now and betray the memory of his beloved master? This Henry was a fine little fellow, but if Willy's words contained even the smallest particle of the truth, then sticking with the boy would be like signing his own death sentence.

Still, he couldn't bring himself to bolt. He had been with Henry for only forty minutes, and already the attachment was too strong for him to dash off without saying good-bye. Torn between fear and affection, he chose a middle course, which was the only course available to him under the circumstances. He simply stopped – just came to a dead halt on the sidewalk, lay down on the ground, and began to whimper. Henry, who had little experience with dogs, had no idea what to make of this sudden, unexpected move. He crouched down beside Mr. Bones and began stroking his head, and the dog, trapped in an agony of indecision, could not help noticing what a gentle touch the boy had.

"You're bushed," Henry said. "Here I am blabbing away, and you're all worn out and hungry, and I haven't even bothered to feed you."

A Big Mac followed, topped off by a bag of fries, and once Mr. Bones had devoured these delectable offerings, his heart was putty in the boy's hands. Run away from this, he told himself, and you'll die in the streets. Go home with him, and you'll die there too. But at least you'll be with Henry, and if death is everywhere, what difference does it make where you go?

And so it was that Mr. Bones went against his master's teachings and wound up living by the gates of hell.

His new home was a cardboard box that had once contained a jumbo-model Fedders air-conditioner. For caution's sake, Henry wedged it between the cyclone fence and one of the old refrigerators in the backyard. That was where Mr. Bones slept at night, curled up in his dark cell until the boy came to fetch him in the morning, and because Henry was a clever lad and had dug a hole under the fence, Mr. Bones could crawl through to the next yard – thus avoiding both the back and side doors of the restaurant – and meet up with his young master at the other end of the block to begin their daily rambles.

Don't think that the dog wasn't afraid, and don't think that he wasn't aware of the perils that surrounded him – but at the same time, know too that he never once regretted his decision to team up with Henry. The restaurant provided him with an inexhaustible source of savory delicacies, and for the first time since *Mom-san*'s death four years earlier, Mr. Bones had enough to eat. Spareribs and dumplings, sesame noodles and fried rice, tofu in brown sauce, braised duck and lighter-than-air won tons: the variety was endless, and once he had been initiated into the glories of Chinese cooking, he could scarcely contain himself at the thought of what Henry would be bringing him next. His stomach had never been happier, and while his digestion sometimes suffered as a result of a too-tangy spice or seasoning, those intermittent bowel eruptions seemed a small price to pay for the pleasure of the meals themselves. If there was any drawback to this heady regime, it was the pang of unknowing that pricked his soul whenever his tongue chanced upon an unidentifiable taste. Willy's prejudices had become his fears, and as he bit down on the obscure new concoction, he couldn't help wondering if he was eating a fellow dog. He would stop chewing then, suddenly frozen with remorse, but it was always too late. His salivary juices were already flowing, and with his taste buds aching for more of what they had only just discovered, his appetite would always get the better of him. After the brief pause, his tongue would dart out at the food again, and before he could tell himself that he was committing a sin, the platter would be licked clean. A moment of sadness would inevitably follow. Then, in an effort to assuage his guilty conscience, he would tell himself that if this was to be his fate as well, he only hoped that he would taste as good as the thing he had just eaten.

Henry bought several packets of radish seeds and planted them in the dirt near Mr. Bones's cardboard box. The garden was his cover story, and whenever his parents asked him why he was spending so much time in the backyard, he had only to mention the radishes and they would nod their heads and walk away. It was peculiar to start a garden so late in the season, his father said, but Henry had already prepared an answer to that question. Radishes germinate in eighteen days, he said, and they would be up long before the weather turned cold. Clever Henry. He could always talk his way out of tricky spots, and with his knack for pinching coins and stray singles from his mother's purse and his night-time raids on the kitchen leftovers, he built a more than tolerable life for himself and his new friend. It wasn't his fault that his father gave Mr. Bones several bad scares by coming out to the garden in the middle of the night to inspect the progress of the radishes. Each time the beam of his flashlight swept over the area in front of Mr. Bones's box, the dog would quake in the darkness of his cubicle, certain that the end was upon him. Once or twice, the stink of fear that rose up from his body was so pungent that Mr. Chow actually stopped to sniff the air, as if suspecting that something was wrong. But he never knew what he was looking for, and after a moment or two of puzzled reflection, he would rattle off a string of incomprehensible Chinese words and then return to the house.

Gruesome as those nights were, Mr. Bones would always forget them the moment he set eyes on Henry in the morning. Their days would begin at the secret corner, directly in front of the trash bin and the coin-operated newspaper dispenser, and for the next eight or ten hours, it was as if the restaurant and the cardboard box were no more than images from a bad dream. They would walk around the city together, drifting from here to there with no special purpose in mind, and the aimlessness of this routine was so like the helter-skelter days with Willy that Mr. Bones had no trouble understanding what was expected of him. Henry was a solitary child, a boy who was used to being alone and living in his thoughts, and now that he had a companion to share his days with, he talked continuously, unburdening himself of the smallest, most ephemeral musings that flitted through his eleven-year-old brain. Mr. Bones loved listening to him, loved the flow of words that accompanied their steps, and in that these monologic free-for-alls reminded him of his dead master as well, he sometimes wondered if Henry Chow were not the true and legitimate heir of Willy G. Christmas, the reincarnated spirit of the one and only himself.

That wasn't to say that Mr. Bones always understood what his new master was talking about, however. Henry's preoccupations were radically different from Willy's, and the dog usually found himself at a loss whenever the boy started in on his pet subjects. How could Mr. Bones be expected to know what an earned-run average was or how many games the Orioles were behind in the standings? In all the years he had spent with Willy, the poet had never once

touched on the topic of baseball. Now, over-
night, it seemed to have become a matter of life
and death. The first thing Henry did every
morning after meeting up with Mr. Bones at
their corner was to put some coins into the newspaper dispenser and buy a copy of *The Baltimore
Sun*. Then, hastening to a bench across the street,
he would sit down, pull out the sports section,
and read an account of the previous night's
game to Mr. Bones. If the Orioles had won, his
voice was full of happiness and excitement. If
the Orioles had lost, his voice was sad and
mournful, at times even tinged with anger. Mr.
Bones learned to hope for wins and to dread the
prospect of losses, but he never quite understood what Henry meant when he talked about
the *team*. An oriole was a bird, not a group of
men, and if the orange creature on Henry's black
cap was indeed a bird, how could it be involved
in something as strenuous and complex as baseball? Such were the mysteries of the new world
he had entered. Orioles fought with tigers, blue
jays battled against angels, bear cubs warred
with giants, and none of it made any sense. A
baseball player was a man, and yet once he
joined a team he was turned into an animal, a
mutant being, or a spirit who lived in heaven
next to God.

According to Henry, there was one bird in the Baltimore flock who stood out from the rest. His name was Cal, and although he was no more than a ball-playing oriole, he seemed to embody the attributes of several other creatures as well: the endurance of a workhorse, the courage of a lion, and the strength of a bull. All that was perplexing enough, but when Henry decided that Mr. Bones's new name should also be Cal – short for Cal Ripken Junior the Second – the dog was thrown into a state of genuine confusion. It's not that he objected to the principle of the thing. He was in no position to tell Henry what his real name was, after all, and since the boy had to call him something, *Cal* seemed as good a name as any other. The only problem was that it rhymed with *Al*, and the first few times he heard Henry say it, he automatically thought of Willy's old friend, dapper Al Saperstein, the man who owned that novelty shop they used to visit on Surf Avenue in Coney Island. He would suddenly see Uncle Al in his mind again, decked out in his lemon-yellow bow tie and hound's-tooth sport jacket, and then he would be back in the shop, watching Willy as he wandered up and down the aisles, perusing the handshake buzzers and whoopee cushions and exploding cigars. He found it painful to encounter Willy like that, to have his old master jump out from the shadows and strut about as if he were still alive, and when you combined these involuntary recollections with Henry's incessant talk about Cal the oriole, and then added in the fact that half the time Henry used the name *Cal* he was actually referring to Mr. Bones, it was hardly strange that the dog wasn't always certain about who he was anymore or what he was supposed to be.

But no matter. He had only just arrived on Planet Henry, and he knew that it would take some time before he felt completely at home there. After one week with the boy, he was already beginning to get the hang of it, and if not for a nasty trick of the calendar, there's no telling what kind of progress they would have made. But summer was not the only season of the year, and with the time approaching for Henry to return to school, the tranquil days of walking and talking and flying kites in the park were suddenly no more. The night before he was to begin the sixth grade, Henry forced himself to stay awake, lying in bed with his eyes open until he was sure his parents were asleep. Just past midnight, when the coast was finally clear, he crept down the back staircase, went into the yard, and climbed into the cardboard box with Mr. Bones. Holding the dog in his arms, he tearfully explained that things were going to be different now. "When the sun comes up in the morning," Henry said, "the fun times will officially be over. I'm such an idiot, Cal. I was going to find another place for you, something better than this rotten box in this rotten backyard, and I didn't do it. I tried, but nobody would help me, and now we've run out of time. You never should have trusted me, Cal. I'm a loser. I'm a retarded piece of shit, and I mess up everything. I always have and I always will. That's what happens when you're a coward. I'm too scared to talk to my dad about you, and if I go behind his back and talk to my mom, she'll just tell him anyway, and that would only make things worse. You're the best friend I've ever had, and all I've done is let you down."

Mr. Bones had only the dimmest idea of what Henry was talking about. The boy was sobbing too hard for his words to be understood, but as the rush of chopped-off syllables and stuttered phrases continued, it became increasingly clear that this outburst was more than just a passing mood. Something was wrong, and while Mr. Bones could scarcely imagine what that thing was, Henry's sadness was beginning to have an effect on him, and within a matter of minutes he had taken on the boy's sadness as his own. Such is the way with dogs. They might not always understand the nuances of their masters' thoughts, but they feel what they feel, and in this case there was no doubt that young Henry Chow was in bad shape. Ten minutes went by, then twenty minutes, then thirty, and there they sat, the boy and the dog, wedged together in the darkness of the cardboard box, the boy with his arms wrapped tightly around the dog, crying his eyes out, and the dog whimpering along in sympathy, raising his head every so often to lick the tears from the boy's face.

Eventually, they both fell asleep. First Henry, then Mr. Bones, and in spite of the somber occasion, in spite of the cramped quarters and the paucity of air that made breathing difficult inside the box, Mr. Bones took courage from the warmth of the body next to him, relishing the fact that he didn't have to spend another terror-filled night alone in the darkness. For the first time since Willy was taken from him, he slept soundly and deeply, untroubled by the dangers that surrounded him.

Dawn broke. Pinkish light filtered through a seam in the cardboard box, and Mr. Bones stirred, struggling to disengage himself from Henry's arms and stretch his body. A few moments of jostling ensued, but even as the dog thrashed about, knocking against the inner walls of the enclosure, the boy slept on, oblivious to all the commotion. It was remarkable how children could sleep, Mr. Bones thought, finally getting himself into a spot where he could flex his knotted muscles, but the hour was still early – just past six o'clock – and given how exhausted he had been after his late-night crying fit, it probably made sense that Henry should still be dead to the world. The dog studied the boy's face in the flickering penumbra – so smooth and round in comparison to Willy's ancient, bearded mug – and watched as little bubbles of saliva dripped down from his tongue and gathered in the corners of his half-open mouth. Tenderness welled up in Mr. Bones's heart. As long as Henry was with him, he realized, he would have been glad to stay in this box for ever.

Ten seconds later, Mr. Bones was jolted from his reverie by a loud thud. The sound came crashing down on him like an explosion, and before he could identify it as a human foot kicking the outside of the box, Henry had opened his eyes and was beginning to scream. Then the box itself was rising off the ground. A rush of early-morning light engulfed Mr. Bones, and for a moment or two it was as if he had gone blind. He heard a man shouting in Chinese, and then, an instant later, the box was flying through the air in the direction of Henry's radish patch. Mr. Chow stood before them, dressed in a sleeveless undershirt and a pair of blue shorts, the veins of his thin neck bulging as the tirade of incomprehensible words continued. He jabbed the air with his finger, again and again pointing it at Mr. Bones, and Mr. Bones barked back at him, confused by the intensity of the man's anger, by the noise of Henry's wailing, by the sudden chaos of the whole hysterical scene. The man lunged at Mr. Bones, but the dog danced back, keeping himself at a safe distance. Then the man went for the boy, who was already trying to escape by crawling through the hole under the fence, and because the boy wasn't fast enough, or because he had started too late, it wasn't long before his father had yanked him to his feet and slapped him across the back of the head. By then, Mrs. Chow had come into the yard as well, charging out the back door in her flannel nightgown, and as Mr. Chow continued to shout at Henry, and as Henry continued to belt out his shrill, soprano screams, Mrs. Chow soon added her own voice to the din, venting her displeasure on both her husband and her son. Mr. Bones retreated to the opposite corner of the yard. By now, he knew that all was lost. Nothing good could come of this battle, at least not as far as he was concerned, and sorry as he felt for Henry, he felt even sorrier for himself. The only solution was to get out of there, to pull up stakes and run.

He waited until the man and the woman started dragging the boy toward the house. When they were within range of the back door, Mr. Bones scampered across the yard and crawled through the hole under the fence. He paused for a moment, waiting for Henry to disappear through the door. Just as the boy was about to go in, however, he broke free of his parents, turned in Mr. Bones's direction, and called out in that anguished, piercing voice of his: "Cal, don't leave me! Don't leave me, Cal!" As if in response to his son's desperation, Mr. Chow picked up a stone from the ground and threw it at Mr. Bones. The dog instinctively jumped back, but the moment he did so, he felt ashamed of himself for not holding his ground. He watched the stone as it clattered harmlessly against the links of the metal fence. Then he barked three times in farewell, hoping the boy would understand that he was trying to speak to him. Mr. Chow opened the door, Mrs. Chow pushed Henry inside, and Mr. Bones began to run.

He had no idea where he was going, but he knew that he couldn't stop, that he had to keep on running until his legs gave out on him or his heart exploded in his chest. If there was any hope for him, any sliver of a chance that he would live beyond the next few days, let alone the next few hours, then he would have to get out of Baltimore. All bad things lived in this city. It was a place of death and despair, of dog-haters and Chinese restaurants, and it was only by the skin of his teeth that he hadn't wound up as a bogus appetizer in a little white takeout box. Too bad about the boy, of course, but given how quickly Mr. Bones had attached himself to his young master, it was remarkable how few regrets he had about leaving. The cardboard box no doubt had something to do with it. The nights he'd spent in there had been almost unendurable, and what good was a home if you didn't feel safe in it, if you were treated as an outcast in the very spot that was supposed to be your refuge? Shutting up a soul in a dark box wasn't right. That's what they did to you after you were dead, but as long as you were alive, as long as you had some kick left in you, you owed it to yourself and everything holy in this world not to submit to such indignities. To be alive meant to breathe; to breathe meant the open air; and the open air meant any place that was not Baltimore, Maryland.

4

He kept on running for three days, and in all that time he barely paused to sleep or look for food. When Mr. Bones finally stopped, he was somewhere in northern Virginia, sprawled out in a meadow ninety miles west of the Chows' backyard. Two hundred yards in front of him, the sun was going down behind a stand of oaks. Half-a-dozen swallows darted back and forth in the middle distance, skimming the field as they combed the air for mosquitoes, and in the darkness of the branches behind him, songbirds chirped out a few last refrains before turning in for the night. As he lay there in the tall grass, his chest heaving and his tongue dangling from his mouth, Mr. Bones wondered what would happen if he closed his eyes – and, if he did, whether he would be able to open them again in the morning. He was that tired and hungry, that muddled by the rigors of his marathon trek. If he fell asleep, it seemed perfectly possible to him that he would never wake up again.

He watched the sun as it continued to sink behind the trees, his eyes struggling to stay open as the darkness gathered around him. He didn't hold out for more than a minute or two, but even before weariness got the better of him, Mr. Bones's head had already begun to fill up with thoughts of Willy, fleeting pictures from the bygone days of smoke rings and Lucky Strikes, the goofball antics of their life together in the world of long ago. It was the first time since his master's death that he had been able to think about such things without feeling crushed by sorrow, the first time he had understood that memory was a place, a real place that one could visit, and that to spend a few moments among the dead was not necessarily bad for you, that it could in fact be a source of great comfort and happiness. Then he fell asleep, and Willy was still there with him, alive again in all his fractured glory, pretending to be a blind man as Mr. Bones led him down the steps of the subway. It was that windy day in March four and a half years ago, he realized, that funny afternoon of high hopes and dashed expectations when they rode out to Coney Island together to unveil the Symphony of Smells to Uncle Al. Willy had donned a Santa Claus hat to mark the occasion, and with the materials for the Symphony crammed inside a huge plastic garbage bag, which he had slung over his shoulder and which made him walk with a stoop, he looked for all the world like some drunk-tank version of Father Christmas himself. It's true that things didn't work out so well once they got there, but that was only because Uncle Al was in a bad mood. He wasn't a real uncle, of course, just a family friend who had lent a helping hand to Willy's parents after they arrived from Poland, and it was only out of some ancient loyalty to *Mom-san* and her husband that he allowed Willy and Mr. Bones to hang around his store. In point of fact, Al had little use for the novelty business, and with fewer and fewer customers showing up to buy his goods, there were certain items that had been languishing on the shelves for ten, twelve, and even twenty years. By now it was no more than a front for his other activities, most of them illegal, some of them not, and if the shady, fast-talking Al hadn't been turning a profit on fireworks, bookmaking, and the sale of stolen cigarettes, he wouldn't have thought twice about closing the door of that dusty emporium for ever. Who knows what scam had backfired on him that windy day in March, but when Willy traipsed in with his Symphony of Smells and started yammering to Uncle Al about how his invention was going to turn them both into millionaires, the proprietor of Whoopee-Land USA turned a deaf ear on his faux nephew's sales pitch. "You're out of your skull, Willy," Uncle Al said, "you're fucking bonkers, you know that?" and promptly shooed him outside with his garbage bag of stinks and smells and collapsible cardboard labyrinths. Not to be dissuaded by a little skepticism, Willy enthusiastically set about to construct the symphony on the sidewalk, determined to prove to Uncle Al that he had indeed come up with one of the genuine marvels of all time. But the air was exceedingly gusty that day, and no sooner did Willy reach into the garbage bag and start pulling out the various elements of *Symphony No. 7* (towels, sponges, sweaters, galoshes, Tupperware boxes, gloves) than the wind caught hold of them and blew them down the street, scattering them in several different directions. Willy ran off to retrieve them, but once he let go of the bag, that too was blown away, and for all his supposed kindness to the Gurevitch family, Uncle Al just stood in the doorway and laughed.

That's what had happened four and a half years ago, but in the dream Mr. Bones had that night in the meadow, he and Willy never got off the subway. There was no question that they were on their way to Coney Island (witness the red-and-white Santa hat, the bulging garbage bag, the seeing-eye dog harness strapped around Mr. Bones's shoulders), but whereas the car of the F train had been quite crowded on the afternoon of the real journey, this time he and Willy were alone, the only two passengers riding out to the end of the line. The moment he became aware of this difference, Willy turned to him and said, "Don't worry, Mr. Bones. It's not then. It's now."

"And what's that supposed to mean?" the dog replied, and so naturally did these words come to him, so clearly were they the product of a long-standing, thoroughly proven ability to speak whenever he had something to say, that Mr. Bones was not the least bit astonished by the miracle that had just occurred.

"It means you're going about it all wrong," Willy said. "Running away from Baltimore, moping around in dumb-ass meadows, starving yourself for no good reason. It just won't do, my friend. You find yourself another master, or your fur is toast."

"I found Henry, didn't I?" Mr. Bones said.

"A plum of a boy, that one, true blue through and through. But not good enough. That's the trouble with young ones. They might mean well, but they don't have any power. You have to go straight to the top, Mr. Bones. Find out who's boss. Find out who makes the decisions, and then attach yourself to that person. There's no other way. You need a new set-up, but it's never going to happen unless you start using your head."

"I was desperate. How could I know his father would turn out to be such a louse?"

"Because I warned you about those places, didn't I? The moment you saw what you were getting yourself into, you should have cashed in your chips and run."

"I did run. And when I wake up tomorrow morning, I'm going to start running again. That's my life now, Willy. I run, and I'm going to keep on running until I drop."

"Don't give up on men, Bonesy. You've had some hard knocks, but you've got to tough it out and give it another try."

"Men can't be trusted. I know that now."

"You trust me, don't you?"

"You're the only one, Willy. But you're not like other men, and now that you're gone, there isn't a place on earth where I'm not in danger. Just yesterday, I nearly got myself shot. I was taking a shortcut through a field somewhere, and a guy came after me in a red pickup truck. Laughing, too, I might add, and then he pulled out a rifle and fired. Lucky for me he missed. But who knows what's going to happen next time?"

"He's just one man. For every person like him, there's another one like Henry."

"Your numbers are off, master. There might be

a few stray fools with a soft spot for dogs, but most of them wouldn't think twice about loading up their shotguns the moment a four-leg sets foot on their land. I'm scared, Willy. Scared to go east, scared to go west. The way things stand now, I think I'd rather starve out here in the wilderness than run into one of those bullets. They'll kill you just for breathing, and when you're up against that kind of hatred, what's the use of trying?"

"All right, give up if you want to. It's no skin off my nose. I could sit here and tell you everything's going to work out, but what's the point of lying to you? Maybe it will, and maybe it won't. I'm no fortune-teller, and the truth is that not all stories have happy endings."

"That's what I've been trying to tell you."

"I know that. And I'm not saying you're wrong."

Until that moment, the train had been speeding through the tunnel at a steady clip, rushing past the empty stations without stopping. Now, suddenly, Mr. Bones heard the screech of brakes, and the train began to slow down. "What's happening?" he said. "Why aren't we going fast anymore?"

"I have to get out," Willy said.

"So soon?"

Willy nodded. "I'm going now," he said, "but

before I leave, I just want to remind you of something you might have forgotten." He was already standing up by then, waiting for the doors to open. "Do you remember *Mom-san*, Mr. Bones?"

"Of course I remember her. What do you take me for?"

"Well, they tried to kill her, too. They hunted her down like a dog, and she had to run for her life. People get treated like dogs, too, my friend, and sometimes they have to sleep in barns and meadows because there's nowhere else for them to go. Before you start feeling too sorry for yourself, just remember that you're not the first dog who's ever been lost."

Sixteen hours later, Mr. Bones was ten miles south of the meadow in which he had dreamed the dream, emerging from a small patch of woods at the edge of a newly built subdivision of two-story houses. He no longer felt afraid. He was hungry, perhaps, and more than a little tired, but the terror that had been growing inside him for the past several days was largely gone. He had no idea why this should be so, but the fact was that he had woken up feeling much better than at any time since Willy's death. He knew that Willy hadn't really been there with him on the subway, and he knew that he couldn't really talk, but in the afterglow of this dream about impossible and beautiful things, he sensed that Willy was still with him, and even if he couldn't be with him, it was as if he were watching him, and even if the eyes that looked down on him were actually inside him, it made no difference in the larger scheme of things, because those eyes were the exact difference between feeling alone in the world and not feeling alone. Mr. Bones was ill-equipped to parse the subtleties of dreams, visions, and other mental phenomena, but he did know for certain that Willy was in Timbuktu, and if he himself had just been with Willy, perhaps that meant the dream had taken him to Timbuktu as well. That would explain, perhaps, why he had suddenly found himself able to speak – after so many years of struggle and failure. And if he had been to Timbuktu once, was it too much to think that he might not be able to go there again – simply by closing his eyes and chancing upon the right dream? It was impossible to say. But there was comfort in that thought, just as there had been comfort in spending that time with his old friend, even if none of it had really happened, even if none of it would ever happen again.

It was three o'clock in the afternoon, and the air was filled with the sounds of lawn mowers, sprinklers, and birds. Far away, on an invisible highway to the north, a dull bee-swarm of traffic pulsed under the suburban landscape. A radio was turned on, and a woman's voice began to sing. Closer by, someone burst out laughing. It sounded like the laugh of a small child, and as Mr. Bones finally came to the end of the woods he had been wandering in for the past half hour, he poked his snout through the twigs and saw that this was indeed the case. A towheaded boy of two or three was sitting on the ground about twelve feet in front of him, pulling up clumps of grass and flinging them into the air. Each time another shower of grass landed on his head, he broke out with a fresh round of giggles, clapping his hands and bouncing up and down as if he had discovered the most brilliant trick in the world. Ten or twelve yards beyond the boy, a girl with glasses was walking back and forth with a doll in her arms, singing softly to the imaginary infant as if she were trying to lull it to sleep. It was difficult to guess how old she was. Somewhere between seven and nine, Mr. Bones thought, but she also could have been a large six or a small ten, not to speak of an even larger five or even smaller eleven. To the left of the girl, a woman in white shorts and a white halter top was crouched over a bed of red and yellow flowers, carefully digging up weeds with a trowel. Her back was turned to Mr. Bones, and because she was wearing a straw hat with an exceedingly broad brim, her entire face was hidden from view. He was reduced to observing the curve of her spine, the freckles on her slender arms, a splash of white knee, but even with just those few elements to go on, he could tell that she wasn't old, no more than twenty-seven or twenty-eight, which probably meant that she was the mother of the two children. Wary of advancing any farther, Mr. Bones remained where he was, watching the scene from his little hideout at the verge of the woods. He had no way of knowing if this family was pro-dog or anti-dog, no way of knowing if they would treat him with kindness or chase him from their property. One thing was certain, however. He had stumbled upon a very handsome lawn. As he stood there looking at the swath of neatly tended green velvet spread out before him, he realized that it didn't take much imagination to know how good it would feel to roll around on that grass and smell the smells that came from it.

Before he could make up his mind about what to do next, the decision was taken out of his hands. The boy tossed two more fistfuls of grass into the air, and this time, instead of falling straight down on top of him as they had done before, a small breeze stirred at just that moment and carried them off in the direction of the woods. The boy turned his head to watch the flight of the green particles, and as his eyes scanned the space between them, Mr. Bones could see his expression change from one of cold, scientific detachment to one of absolute surprise. The dog had been discovered. The boy shot to his feet and began charging toward him, squealing with happiness as he waddled forth in his bloated plastic diaper, and right then and there, with his whole future suddenly on the line, Mr. Bones decided that this was the moment he had been waiting for. Not only did he not back off into the woods, and not only did he not run away, but in his calmest, most self-assured manner, he gingerly stepped out on to the grass and let the boy throw his arms around him. "Doggy!" the little man cried, squeezing for all he was worth. "Good doggy. Big old funny doggy."

The girl came next, running across the lawn with the doll in her arms and calling out to the woman behind her. "Look, Mama," she said. "Look what Tiger found." Even as the boy went on hugging him, a wave of alarm passed through Mr. Bones's body. Where was this tiger she was talking about – and how could a tiger be prowling around out here where people lived? Willy had taken him to a zoo once, and he knew all about those big striped jungle cats. They were even bigger than lions, and if you ever met up with one of those sharp-fanged babies, you could kiss your future good-bye. A tiger would rip you to shreds in about twelve seconds, and whatever bits of you he didn't feel like eating would be fine stuff for the vultures and worms.

Still, Mr. Bones didn't run away. He continued to let his new friend cling to him, patiently bearing the brunt of the tyke's phenomenal strength, and hoped that his ears had been playing tricks on him, that he'd simply misheard what the girl had said. The sagging diaper was loaded with urine, and mingled in with the sharp ammonia scent he could detect traces of carrots, bananas, and milk. Then the girl was crouching down beside them, peering into Mr. Bones's face with her blue, magnified eyes, and the mystery was suddenly cleared up. "Tiger," she said to the boy, "let go of him. You'll choke him to death."

"My buddy," Tiger said, tightening his grip even more, and although Mr. Bones was gratified to discover that he wasn't about to be devoured by a wild beast, the pressure on his throat was becoming severe enough to make him squirm now. The boy might not have been a real tiger, but that didn't mean he wasn't dangerous. In his own little way, he was more of an animal than Mr. Bones was.

Fortunately, the woman arrived just then and grabbed hold of the boy's arm, pulling him off Mr. Bones before more damage could be done. "Careful, Tiger," she said. "We don't know if he's nice dog or not."

"Oh, he's nice," the girl said, gently patting Mr. Bones on his crown. "All you have to do is look into his eyes. He's real nice, Mama. I'd say he's about the nicest dog I've ever seen."

Mr. Bones was stunned by the girl's extraordinary statement, and just to show what a good sport he was, that he was indeed a dog who didn't bear grudges, he began licking Tiger's face in a great burst of slobbering affection. The little fellow howled with laughter, and even though the thrust of Mr. Bones's tongue eventually made him lose his balance, the rough-and-tumble Tiger thought it was the funniest thing that had ever happened to him, and he went on laughing under the barrage of the dog's kisses even as he thudded to the ground on his wet bottom.

"Well, at least he's friendly," the woman said to her daughter, as if conceding an important point. "But what an unholy mess. I don't think I've ever seen a dirtier, scruffier, more dilapidated creature than this one."

"There's nothing wrong with him that a little soap and water can't fix," the girl said. "Just look at him, Mama. He's not just nice, he's smart, too."

The woman laughed. "How can you know that, Alice? He hasn't done a thing but lick your brother's face."

Alice squatted down in front of Mr. Bones and cupped his jowls in her hands. "Show us how smart you are, old boy," she said. "Do a trick or something, okay? You know, like rolling over or standing up on your hind legs. Show Mama that I'm right."

These were hardly difficult tasks for a dog of his mettle, and Mr. Bones promptly set about to demonstrate what he could do. First, he rolled over on the grass – not once but three times – and then he arched his back, lifted his front paws up to his face, and slowly rose up on his hind legs. It had been years since he had tried this last stunt, but even though his joints ached and he tottered more than he would have liked, he managed to hold the position for three or four seconds.

"See, Mama? What did I tell you?" Alice said. "He's the smartest dog that ever was."

The woman crouched down to Mr. Bones's level for the first time and looked into his eyes, and even though she was wearing sunglasses and still had the straw hat on her head, he could see that she was ever so pretty, with wisps of blond hair curling down the back of her neck and a full, expressive mouth. Something shuddered inside him when she spoke to him in her slow, drawling Southern voice, and when she began patting his head with her right hand, Mr. Bones felt that surely his heart would break into a thousand pieces.

"You understand what we're saying to you, don't you, old dog?" she said. "You're a special one, aren't you? And you're tired and beat-up, and you need something to put in your belly. That's it, old-timer, isn't it? You're lost and alone, and every inch of you is tuckered out."

Had a poor mutt ever been luckier than Mr. Bones was that afternoon? Without any further discussion, and without any further need to charm them or prove what a good soul he was, the weary dog was led from the yard into the sanctum of the family house. There, in a radiant white kitchen, surrounded by freshly painted cabinets and shining metal utensils and an air of opulence he had never even imagined could exist on earth, Mr. Bones ate his fill, gorging himself on leftover slices of roast beef, a bowl of macaroni and cheese, two cans of tuna fish, and three uncooked hot dogs, not to mention lapping up two and a half bowls of water in between courses as well. He had wanted to hold back, to show them that he was a dog of modest appetites, really no trouble to take care of, but once the food was set down in front of him his hunger was simply too overpowering, and he forgot the vow he had made.

None of this seemed to bother his hosts. They were good-hearted people, and they knew a hungry dog when they saw one, and if Mr. Bones was that famished, then they were perfectly happy to provide for him until he wasn't. He ate in a trance of contentment, oblivious to everything but the food going into his mouth and sliding down his throat. When the meal was finally over and he looked up to check on what the others were doing, he saw that the woman had removed her hat and sunglasses. As she bent down near him to lift the bowls from the floor, he caught a glimpse of her gray-blue eyes and understood that she was in fact a great beauty, one of those women who made men stop breathing the moment they walked into a room.

"Well, old dog," she said, running her palm over the top of his head, "feeling better?"

Mr. Bones let out a small belch of appreciation, and then he started licking her hand. Tiger, whom he had all but forgotten by then, suddenly came rushing toward him. Drawn by the sound of the belch, which had greatly amused him, the boy leaned forward into Mr. Bones's face and let out a pretend belch of his own, which amused him even more. It was shaping up into another wild barroom scene, but before the situation could get out of hand, his mother swept him into her arms and stood up. She looked over at Alice, who was leaning against a counter and scrutinizing Mr. Bones with her serious, watchful eyes. "What are we going to do with him, baby?" the woman said.

"I think we should keep him," Alice answered.

"We can't do that. He probably belongs to somebody. If we kept him, it would be just like stealing."

"I don't think he has a friend in the world. Just look at him. He's probably walked a thousand miles. If we don't take him in, he's going to die. Do you want that on your conscience, Mama?"

This girl certainly had the gift, all right. She knew just what to say and when to say it, and as Mr. Bones stood there listening to her talk to her mother, he wondered if Willy hadn't underestimated the power of some children. Alice might not have been the boss, and she might not have made the decisions, but her words cut straight to the truth, and that was bound to have an effect, to steer things in one direction rather than another.

"Check his collar, sweetheart," the woman

said. "Maybe there's a name or an address on it or something."

Mr. Bones knew full well that there wasn't, since Willy had never bothered with such things as licenses or registrations or fancy metal name tags. Alice knelt down beside him and began turning the collar around his neck, searching for signs of his identity or ownership, and because he already knew what the answer would be, he took advantage of the moment to enjoy the warmth of her breath as it fluttered against the back of his right ear.

"No, Mama," she said at last. "It's just a plain old ratty collar."

For the first time in the short while he had known her, the dog saw the woman hesitate, and a certain confusion and sadness crept into her eyes. "It's okay by me, Alice," she said. "But I can't give the thumbs-up until we've talked to your father. You know how he hates surprises. We'll wait until he comes home this evening, and then we'll all decide together. Okay?"

"Okay," Alice said, somewhat deflated by this inconclusive response. "But it's three against one, even if he says no. And fair is fair, right? We've just got to keep him, Mama. I'll get down on my knees and pray to Jesus for the rest of the day if it'll make Daddy say yes."

"You don't have to do that," the woman said. "If you really want to help, you'll open the door and let the dog outside so he can do his business. And then we'll see if we can't clean him up a bit. That's the only way this thing is ever going to work. He's got to make a good first impression."

The door opened for Mr. Bones not a moment too soon. After three days of privation, of eating no more than thimblefuls of scraps and garbage, of rooting around for whatever noxious edibles he could find, the richness of the meal he had just consumed hit his stomach with the force of a trauma, and with his digestive juices in full operation again, working double and even triple overtime to accommodate the recent onslaught, it was all he could do not to foul the kitchen floor and be banished into permanent exile. He trotted off behind a clump of bushes, trying to keep himself out of sight, but Alice followed him over, and to his never-ending shame and embarrassment, she was there to witness the dreadful explosion of brackish liquid that roared out of his bunghole and splattered on to the foliage beneath him. She let out a brief gasp of disgust when it happened, and he felt so mortified at offending her that for a moment or two he wished that he could shrivel up and die. But Alice was no ordinary person, and even though he thoroughly understood that by now, he never would have thought it possible for her to say what she said next. "Poor dog," she muttered, in a doleful, pitying voice. "You're awfully sick, aren't you?" That was the entire statement – just two short sentences – but when Mr. Bones heard Alice say those words, he realized that Willy G. Christmas was not the only two-leg in the world who could be trusted. It turned out that there were others, and some of them were very small.

The rest of the afternoon rolled by in a blur of pleasures. They washed him down with the garden hose, lathering his fur into a mountainous pile of white suds, and as the six hands of his new companions rubbed away at his back and chest and head, he couldn't help remembering how the day had begun – and what an odd and mysterious thing it was that it should end like this. Then they rinsed him off, and after he shook himself dry and ran around the yard for a few minutes, peeing on various bushes and trees along the perimeter of the property, the woman sat with him for what seemed like the longest time, searching his body for ticks. She explained to Alice that her father had taught her how to do this in North Carolina when she was a girl and that the only foolproof method was to use your fingernails and pinch out the critters by the tops of their heads. Once you had them, you couldn't just flick them to the side, and you couldn't just crush them underfoot. You had to burn them, and while she was in no way encouraging Alice to play with matches, would she be so kind as to run into the kitchen and fetch the box of Ohio Blue Tips in the top drawer to the right of the stove? Alice did as she was asked, and for the next little while she and her mother combed through Mr. Bones's fur together, plucking out a succession of blood-swollen ticks and incinerating the culprits in little blazes of bright, phosphorescent heat. How not to be grateful for that? How not to rejoice at having this scourge of agonizing itches and sores removed from his person? Mr. Bones was so relieved by what they were doing for him that he even let Alice's next remark pass by without protest. He knew the insult was unintentional, but that didn't mean he wasn't hurt by it.

"I don't want to get your hopes up too high," the woman said to her, "but it might not be such a bad idea to give this dog a name before your daddy gets home. It'll make him seem more like part of the family, and that might give us a psychological edge. You understand what I'm saying, honey?"

"I already know his name," Alice said. "I

knew it the moment I saw him." The girl paused for a moment to collect her thoughts. "Remember that book you used to read to me when I was little? The red one with the pictures in it and all those stories about animals? There was a dog in there that looked just like this one. He rescued a baby from a burning building and could count up to ten. Remember, Mama? I used to love that dog. When I saw Tiger hugging this one by the bushes a little while ago, it was like a dream come true."

"What was his name?"

"Sparky. His name was Sparky the Dog."

"All right, then. We'll call this one Sparky, too."

When Mr. Bones heard the woman go along with this absurd choice, he felt stung. It had been bad enough trying to get used to *Cal*, but this was pushing things a little too far. He had suffered too much to be burdened with this cutesy, infantile nickname, this simpering diminutive inspired by a picture book for toddlers, and even if he lived as long again as he had lived so far, he knew that a dog of his melancholic temperament would never adjust to it, that he would cringe every time he heard it for the rest of his days.

Before Mr. Bones could work himself into a real snit, however, trouble broke out in another area of the yard. For the past ten minutes, as Alice and her mother picked away at the vermin embedded in his coat, Mr. Bones had been watching Tiger entertain himself by kicking a beach ball across the lawn. Each time it squirted away from him, he would run after it at top speed, looking like a demented soccer player in pursuit of a ball twice his size. The kid was tireless, but that didn't mean he couldn't trip and stub his toe, and when the inevitable accident finally occurred, he let out a shriek of pain that was loud enough to drive the sun from the sky and bring the clouds crashing down to the earth. The woman left off from her delicate ministrations to take care of the boy, and as she picked him up and carried him off into the house, Alice turned to Mr. Bones and said, "That's Tiger. Nine tenths of the time, he's either laughing or crying, and when he isn't, you can be pretty sure that something weird is about to happen. You'll get used to it, Sparky. He's only two and a half, and you can't expect too much from little boys. His real name is Terry, but we all call him Tiger because he's such a roughhouser. My name is Alice. Alice Elizabeth Jones. I'm eight and three-quarters, and I just started the fourth grade. I was born with little holes in my heart, and I almost died a couple of times when I was small, even smaller than Tiger is now. I don't remember any of that, but Mama said I lived because I have an angel breathing inside me, and that angel is going to keep on protecting me for ever. Mama's name is Polly Jones. She used to be Polly Danforth, but then she married Daddy and changed her name to Jones. My daddy is Richard Jones. Everyone calls him Dick, and most people say I look more like him than I look like Mama. He's an airline pilot. He flies to California and Texas and New York, all kinds of places. Once, before Tiger was born, Mama and I got to go to Chicago with him. Now we're living in this big house. We just moved in a few months ago, so it's a lucky thing you came when you did, Sparky. We've got plenty of room, and we're all settled in now, and if Daddy says we can keep you, then everything will be just about perfect around here."

She was trying to make him feel welcome, but the net effect of Alice's rambling introduction to the family was to throw Mr. Bones into panic and turn his stomach inside out. His future was in the hands of a person he had never seen, and after listening to the various comments that had been made about this person so far, it seemed unlikely that the decision would come down in the dog's favor. The force of these anxieties sent Mr. Bones running into the bushes again, and for the second time in an hour his intestines betrayed him. Trembling uncontrollably as the crap gushed on to the ground, he begged the god of dogdom to take care of his poor, sick body. He had entered the promised land, had fallen into a world of green lawns and gentle women and abundant food, but if it came to pass that he should be expelled from this place, then he asked only that his miseries not be prolonged beyond what he could endure.

By the time Dick's Volvo pulled into the driveway, Polly had already fed the children their dinner – hamburgers, baked potatoes, and frozen peas, some of which found its way into Mr. Bones's mouth – and the four of them were out in the yard again, watering the garden as the late afternoon turned into early evening and the sky filled with the first mottled touches of darkness. Mr. Bones had overheard Polly tell Alice that the flight from New Orleans was due in at Dulles at four forty-five, and if the plane wasn't delayed and the traffic wasn't too heavy, her father should be home by seven o'clock. Give or take a few minutes, that's just when Dick Jones arrived. He had been gone for three days, and when the children heard the sound of his approaching car, they both ran screaming from the yard and vanished around the side of the house. Polly made no move to run after them. She calmly went on watering her plants and flowers, and Mr. Bones stuck by her, unwilling to let her out of his sight. He knew that all hope was gone now, but if anybody could save him from the thing that was about to happen, she was the one.

A few moments later, the man of the house walked into the yard with Tiger in one arm and Alice tugging on the other, and because he was wearing his pilot's uniform (dark-blue pants; light-blue shirt garnished with epaulets and insignias), Mr. Bones mistook him for a cop. It was an automatic association, and with a lifetime of dread built into that response, he couldn't help recoiling as Dick approached, even though he could see with his own eyes that the man was laughing and seemed genuinely happy to be with his children again. Before Mr. Bones could sort through this jumble of doubts and conflicting impressions, he was swept up into the drama of the moment, and from then on everything seemed to happen at once. Alice had started talking to her father about the dog the instant he stepped out of the car, and she was still at it when he entered the yard and greeted his wife (a perfunctory kiss on the cheek), and the more she badgered him and raved on about the wonderful creature they had found, the more excited her little brother became. Yelling "Sparky" at the top of his lungs, Tiger slithered out of his father's grasp, ran over to Mr. Bones, and threw his arms around his neck. Not to be outdone by her pipsqueak brother, Alice came over and got into the act as well, making a great, histrionic show of affection for the dog as she attacked him with repeated hugs and melodramatic kisses, and with the two kids suddenly mauling him like that and covering his ears with their hands and chests and faces, he missed three-quarters of what the adults were saying. About the only thing he heard with any clarity was Dick's initial statement. "So this is the famous dog, huh? Looks like one sorry mutt to me."

After that, it was anyone's guess as to what really happened. He saw Polly twist the nozzle of the hose, which cut off the flow of water, and then she said something to Dick. Most of it was inaudible, but from the few words and phrases that Mr. Bones managed to catch, he understood that she was pleading his case: "wandered into the yard this afternoon," "intelligent," "the kids think . . .", and then, after Dick said something back to her, "I don't have the foggiest idea. Maybe he ran away from the circus." It sounded fairly encouraging, but just as he succeeded in getting his left ear free of Tiger's grip to take in a little more, Polly tossed the hose on to the ground and wandered off with Dick in the direction of the house. They stopped a few feet in front of the back door and went on talking there. Mr. Bones was certain that momentous things were being decided now, but even though their lips were moving, he could no longer hear a word they said.

He could see that Dick was watching him, however, gesturing toward him every now and then with a vague sweep of the hand as he continued his discussion with Polly, and Mr. Bones, who was growing a little bored with the raucous love-in that Tiger and Alice had started, wondered if it might not be such a bad idea to take the initiative and do something to help himself. Instead of standing around while his future hung in the balance, why not try to impress Dick with some canine derring-do, some spiffy dog thing that would turn the tide in his favor? It was true that Mr. Bones was exhausted, and it was true that his stomach still hurt and his legs felt diabolically weak, but he didn't let those things stop him from bounding off and racing to the other end of the yard. Shrieking with surprise, Tiger and Alice went running after him, and just as they were about to catch him, he bounded away from them again, abruptly charging back in the direction he had come from. Again they went after him, and again he waited until they almost had him in their hands before jumping away. He hadn't sprinted like that in aeons, but even though he knew that he was pushing himself too hard and would eventually have to pay for his exertions, he kept on going, proud to be torturing himself on behalf of such a noble cause. After three or four dashes across the lawn, he stopped in the middle of the yard and played duck-and-feint with them – the dog version of tag – and even though he could barely breathe anymore, he refused to quit before the children gave up and flopped to the ground in front of him.

Meanwhile, the sun was beginning to go down. The sky was streaked with bands of pinkish clouds, and the air had turned cooler. Now that the romp-a-thon had ended, it appeared that Dick and Polly were ready to announce their verdict. As Mr. Bones lay panting on the grass with the two children, he saw the grown-ups turn from the house and begin walking back to the yard, and while it was never clear to him whether his manic burst of high spirits had any effect on the outcome, he took heart from the satisfied little smile that was creasing the edges of Polly's mouth. "Daddy says that Sparky can stay," she said, and as Alice jumped up from the ground and hugged her father and Polly bent down and gathered the half-sleeping Tiger into her arms, a new chapter in Mr. Bones's life began.

Before they could break out the champagne, however, Dick butted in with a few additional points – the fine print, so to speak. It's not that he didn't want everyone to be happy, he said, but for the time being it had to be understood that they were only keeping the dog on a "trial basis," and unless certain conditions were met – and here he gave Alice a long, hard look – the deal was off. First: under no circumstances was the dog to be allowed in the house. Second: he would have to be taken to the vet for a full checkup. If he wasn't found to be in reasonably good health, he would have to go. Third: at the earliest possible convenience, an appointment would have to be made with a professional groomer. The dog needed a haircut, a shampoo, and a manicure, as well as a thorough going-over for ticks, lice, and fleas. Fourth: he would have to be fixed. And fifth: Alice would be responsible for feeding him and changing his water bowl – with no increase in her allowance for services rendered.

Mr. Bones had no idea what the word *fixed* meant, but he understood everything else, and all in all it didn't sound too bad, except maybe for the first point about not being allowed in the house, since he failed to grasp how a dog could become part of a family's household if he didn't have the right to enter that family's house. Alice must have been wondering the same thing, for as soon as her father came to the last item on his list, she chimed in with a question. "What happens when winter comes?" she asked. "We're not going to leave him out here in the cold, are we, Daddy?"

"Of course not," Dick said. "We'll put him in the garage, and if it's still too cold in there, we'll let him stay in the cellar. I just don't want him getting his hair all over the furniture, that's all. But we'll make it real nice for him out here, don't worry. We'll give him a first-class doghouse, and I'll set up a run for him by stringing a wire between those two trees over there. He'll have plenty of space to frisk about in, and once he gets used to it, he'll be happy as a clam. Don't feel sorry for him, Alice. He's not a person, he's a dog, and dogs don't ask questions. They make do with what they get." With that decisive remark, Dick put his hand on Mr. Bones's head and gave it a firm, manly squeeze, as if to prove he wasn't such an ornery customer after all. "Ain't that right, sport?" he said. "You're not going to complain, are you? You know what you've lucked into here, and the last thing you want is to rock the boat."

He was a can-do guy, this Dick, and even though the next day was Sunday – which meant that both the groomer and the vet were closed – he got up early, drove off to the lumberyard in Polly's van, and then spent the entire morning and afternoon putting together a pre-fab dog-house (deluxe model, assembly instructions included) and rigging up a run in the backyard. He clearly belonged to that class of men who felt happier lugging around ladders and hammering nails into boards than making small talk with his wife and children. Dick was a man of action, a soldier in the war against idleness, and as Mr. Bones watched him working away in his khaki shorts and saw the sweat glistening on his fore-head, he couldn't help but read this activity as a good sign. It meant that all that "trial basis" talk from yesterday had been no more than a bluff. Dick had shelled out over two hundred dollars for this new equipment and hardware. He had toiled in the heat for the better part of a day, and he wasn't about to let his work or money go to waste. His toes were in the water now, and as far as Mr. Bones could tell, it was either sink or swim from this point on.

The next morning, they all flew off in different

directions. A bus stopped in front of the house at quarter to eight and took Alice to school. Forty minutes after that, Dick left for the airport in his pilot's uniform, and then, shortly before nine, Polly strapped Tiger into his child-restraint seat in the van and drove him to his morning play group. Mr. Bones could scarcely believe what was happening. Was this what life was going to be like around here?, he wondered. Were they simply going to abandon him in the morning and expect him to fend for himself all day? It felt like an obscene joke. He was a dog built for companion-ship, for the give-and-take of life with others, and he needed to be touched and spoken to, to be part of a world that included more than just himself. Had he walked to the ends of the earth and found this blessed haven only to be spat on by the peo-ple who had taken him in? They had turned him into a prisoner. They had chained him to this infernal bouncing wire, this metallic torture device with its incessant squeaks and echoing hums, and every time he moved, the noises moved with him – as if to remind him that he was no longer free, that he had sold his birthright for a mess of porridge and an ugly, ready-made house.

Just when it looked as if he might go ahead and do some rash, vindictive thing – like digging up the flowers in the garden, for instance, or

gnawing off the bark of the young cherry tree –
Polly came back, unexpectedly pulling into the
driveway with her van, and the world changed
color again. Not only did she come out to the
yard and release him from his bondage, and not
only did she let him follow her into the house
and go upstairs to her bedroom, but as she
changed her clothes and brushed her hair and
put on her makeup, she informed him that there
were going to be two sets of rules for him to
remember: Dick's rules and her rules. When Dick
was around, Mr. Bones would be confined to the
outdoors, but when Dick was gone, she was in
charge, and that meant that dogs were allowed in
the house. "It's not that he doesn't mean well,"
Polly said, "but that man can be a squarehead
sometimes, and once he's got his brain fixed on
something, you're just wasting your breath if you
try to talk him out of it. That's life with the
Joneses, Sparky, and there's not a damn thing I
can do about it. All I ask is that you keep this little arrangement under your hat. It's our secret,
and not even the kids can know what we're up
to. You hear me, old dog? This is strictly between
you and me."

But that wasn't all. As if this declaration of sol-
idarity and affection hadn't been enough, later
that same morning Mr. Bones got to ride in a car

for the first time in nearly two years. Not scrunched up in the floor in back, where he had usually been put in the past, but right up front in the copilot's seat, riding shotgun with the window open and the sweet Virginia air rushing in on his face. It was a sublime vindication to be tooling down the road like that, with the magnificent Polly at the wheel of the Plymouth Voyager and the motion of the van rumbling inside his muscles and his nose twitching crazily at each passing smell. When it finally hit him that this van was going to be a part of his new routine, he was awed by the prospect that loomed before him. Life with Willy had been good, but maybe this was even better. For the sad truth was that poets didn't drive, and even when they traveled on foot, they didn't always know where they were going.

The visit to the groomer's was something of an ordeal, but he bore up to the multiple assaults of soaps and shears as best he could, not wanting to complain after all the kindness that had been bestowed on him. When they finished with him an hour and a half later, he emerged as an altogether different dog. Gone were the shaggy clumps of fur dangling from his hocks, the messy protrusions jutting from his withers, the hair hanging in his eyes. He was no longer a bum, no longer an embarrassment. He had been dandi-fied, turned into a bourgeois dog-about-town, and if the novelty of the transformation made him want to gloat and preen a little bit, who could blame him for exulting in his good for-tune? "Wow," Polly said when they finally took him out to her. "They sure gave you the once-over, didn't they? Next thing you know, Spark Plug, you'll be winning prizes at the dog shows."

Twenty-four hours later, they went to see the vet. Mr. Bones was glad for the chance to ride in the car again, but he'd crossed paths with those men in the white coats before, and he knew enough about their needles and thermometers and rubber gloves to dread what was coming. Mrs. Gurevitch had always been the one to schedule his appointments in the past, but after she died, Mr. Bones had been spared the agony of further dealings with the medical profession. Willy had been either too broke or too forgetful to bother anymore, and since the dog was still alive after four years of not going to the doctor, he failed to see what good a checkup was going to do him now. If you were sick enough to die, a doctor wasn't going to save you. And if you weren't sick, why let them torture you with their pricking and poking only to be told that your health was okay?

It would have been a horror if Polly hadn't stayed with him during the examination, holding him in her arms and soothing him with her soft, lovely voice. Even with her help, he trembled and shook throughout the entire visit, and three times he jumped off the table and ran for the door. The doctor's name was Burnside, Walter A. Burnside, and it made no difference that the quack seemed to like him. Mr. Bones had seen him looking at Polly, and he had smelled the arousal on the young doctor's skin. She was the one he was after, and liking her dog was only a ruse, a way to get on her good side and impress her with his understanding and skill. It didn't matter that he called Mr. Bones a wise dog and patted him on the head and laughed at his attempts to escape. He did it so he could get closer to Polly, maybe even brush up against her body, and Polly, who was so absorbed in taking care of the dog, didn't even notice what the scoundrel was up to.

"Not bad," the doctor said at last. "Considering what he's been through."

"He's a tough old trouper," Polly said, giving Mr. Bones a kiss between the eyes. "But his stomach is shot. I hate to think about some of the things that must have gone in there."

"He'll be all right once you get him on a regular diet. And don't forget to give him the worm pills. In a week or two, you'll probably start to see a big improvement."

Polly thanked the doctor, and when she and Burnside shook hands on her way out, Mr. Bones couldn't help noticing that Señor Smooth held on longer than he should have. When he answered Polly's polite good-bye by saying "The pleasure's been all mine," the dog had a sudden urge to jump up and bite him on the leg. Polly turned to leave. Just as she was opening the door, the doctor added: "Talk to June at the front desk. She'll schedule you in for the other matter."

"It wasn't my idea," Polly said. "But that's the way my husband wants it."

"He's right," Burnside said. "It simplifies things, and in the long run it'll make Sparky a whole lot happier."

Dick returned home on Thursday night, which meant that Friday morning was much duller than the previous mornings had been. No more stealthy, luxurious hours spent in the house. No more sitting in the bathroom and watching Polly take her bath. No more scrambled eggs. No more sugary milk from the children's cereal bowls. Ordinarily, losses of that magnitude would have pained him, but on that particular Friday morning they produced no more than a stab of wistful regret. Mr. Bones had hope now, and he knew that once Dick left on Sunday afternoon, the door would open for him again. There was solace in this thought, and even though it was drizzling that day and the air had turned cool with the first traces of autumn, he settled into his doghouse with the rubber bone that Polly had bought for him at the groomer's and nibbled away at it as the family ate breakfast inside. He heard the bus come and go, he heard the van drive off, and then, in the interval before Polly returned, Dick sauntered out into the yard to say hello. Not even that could ruffle his contentment. The pilot seemed to be in a chipper mood that morning, and when he complimented Mr. Bones on his fine haircut and asked him how he was getting along, the dog's generosity won out over his suspicions, and he responded with a discreet, gentlemanly lick of the hand. It wasn't that he was against Dick, he decided. It was just that he pitied him for not knowing how to enjoy life. The world was filled with such wonders, and it was a sad state of affairs when a man spent his time worrying about the wrong things.

Mr. Bones was anticipating a long, slow time of it, and he had prepared himself to while away the hours before the children came home by doing as little as possible: dozing, chewing on the bone, strolling around the yard if the rain let up. Indolence was the only chore on the agenda, but Dick kept mentioning what a big day it was, kept harping on how "the moment of truth had finally come," and after a while Mr. Bones began to wonder if he hadn't missed something. He had no idea what Dick was talking about, but after all these mysterious pronouncements, it didn't surprise him that once Polly returned from dropping off Tiger, he was asked to jump into the van and take another ride. It was different, of course, now that Dick was there, but who was he to object to a slight change of protocol? Dick was in the driver's seat, Polly sat next to him, and Mr. Bones rode in back, lying on a beach towel that Dick had put down to protect the car from errant dog hairs. The window couldn't be lowered in back, which reduced the pleasure of the ride considerably, but still, he enjoyed the motion for its own sake, and all in all he much preferred being where he was to where he had been.

He could sense that all was not calm between the Joneses, however. As the ride continued, it became clear that Polly was unusually subdued, gazing out the window to her right instead of looking at Dick, and after a while her silence seemed to dampen Dick's spirits as well.

"Look, Polly," he said, "I'm sorry. But it's really for his own good."

"I don't want to talk about it," she said. "Your mind's made up, and that's the end of it. You know my opinion, so what's the point of arguing anymore?"

"It's not like I'm the only one who ever thought of it," Dick said. "It's common practice."

"Oh yeah? And how would you like it if someone did it to you?"

Dick made a sound that fell halfway between a grunt and a laugh. "Come on, honey, cut it out. He's a dog. He won't even know what happened to him."

"Please, Dick. I don't want to talk about it."

"Why not? If you're so upset —"

"No. Not in front of him. It's not fair."

Dick laughed again, but this time it came out as a kind of uproarious stupefaction, a great guffaw of disbelief. "You've got to be joking!" he said. "I mean, Jesus Christ, Polly, we're talking about a dog!"

"Think what you like. But I'm not going to say another word about it in this car."

And she didn't. But enough had been said for Mr. Bones to start worrying, and when the car finally came to a stop and he saw that they had pulled up in front of the same building he and

Polly had visited on Tuesday morning, the same building that housed the offices of one Walter A. Burnside, doctor of veterinary medicine, he knew that something terrible was about to happen to him.

And it did. And the odd thing about it was that Dick had been right. Mr. Bones never knew what hit him. They put him under with a needle to the rump, and after the excision had been performed and he was led back to the van, he was still too wobbly to know where he was – let alone who he was, or if he was. It was only later, when the anesthetic had worn off, that he began to feel the pain that had been inflicted on him, but even then he remained in the dark as to what had caused it. He knew where it was coming from, but that wasn't the same thing as knowing why it was there, and although he had every intention of examining the spot, he put it off for the time being, realizing that he lacked the strength to contort his body into the proper position. He was already in his doghouse then, stretched out dreamily on his left side, and Polly was on her knees in front of the open door, stroking his head and feeding him from her hand – chopped-up bits of medium-rare steak. The meat had an extraordinary flavor, but the truth was that he didn't have much of an appetite at that moment, and if he accepted what he was given, it was only to please her. The rain had stopped by then. Dick was off with Tiger somewhere, and Alice was still away at school, but being with Polly was comfort enough, and as she continued to stroke his head and assure him that everything was going to be all right, he wondered what the hell had happened to him and why he hurt so much.

In due time, he explored the damage and discovered what was missing, but because he was a dog and not a biologist or a professor of anatomy, he still had no idea what had happened to him. Yes, it was true that the sac was empty now and his old familiars were gone, but what exactly did that mean? He had always enjoyed licking that part of himself, had in fact made a regular habit of it for as long as he could remember, but aside from the tender globes themselves, everything else in the area seemed to be intact. How was he to know that those missing parts had been responsible for turning him into a father many times over? Except for his ten-day affair with Greta, the malamute from Iowa City, his romances had always been brief – impetuous couplings, impromptu flings, frantic rolls in the hay – and he had never seen any of the pups he had sired. And even if he had, how would he have been able to make the connection? Dick

Jones had turned him into a eunuch, but in his own eyes he was still the prince of love, the lord of the canine Romeos, and he would go on courting the ladies until his last, dying breath. For once, the tragic dimension of his own life eluded him. The only thing that mattered was the physical pain, and once that disappeared, he never gave the operation another thought.

More days passed. He settled into the rhythms of the household, grew accustomed to the various comings and goings around him, came to understand the difference between the weekdays and the weekends, the sound of the school bus as opposed to the sound of the UPS truck, the smells of the animals who lived in the woods that bordered the yard: squirrels, raccoons, chipmunks, rabbits, all manner of birds. He knew by now that birds weren't worth the trouble, but whenever a wingless creature wandered on to the lawn, he took it upon himself to chase the varmint from the property, rushing toward him in a frenzied outburst of barks and growls. Sooner or later, they would catch on to the fact that he was hooked up to that damned wire, but for now most of them were sufficiently intimidated by his presence to keep the game interesting. Except for the cat, of course, but that was always the case with cats, and the black one from next door had already figured out the exact length of the leash that held him to the wire, which meant that he knew the limits of Mr. Bones's mobility at every point in the yard. The feline intruder would always position himself in a spot designed to cause the maximum frustration: a few inches out of the dog's range. There was nothing Mr. Bones could do about it. He could either stand there and bark his head off as the cat hissed at him and shot his claws toward his face, or he could retreat into his doghouse and pretend to ignore the cat, even though the son of a bitch would then hop on to the roof and start digging his claws into the dense cedar shingles just above his head. Those were the alternatives: be scratched or be mocked, and either way it was a losing proposition. On the other hand, there were certain small miracles to be seen from that same doghouse, especially at night. A silver fox, for example, who scampered across the lawn at three AM and disappeared before Mr. Bones could stir a muscle, imprinting an afterimage on his mind that was so sharp, so crystalline in its perfection, that it kept coming back to him for days afterward: an apparition of weightlessness and speed, the grace of the wholly wild. And then, on a night in late September, there was the deer who stepped out of the woods, tiptoed around the grass for twenty or thirty seconds, and then, startled by the noise of a distant car, bounded off into the darkness again, leaving great divots in the lawn that were still there the following week.

Mr. Bones grew exceedingly fond of that lawn – the tufted, padded feel of it, the grasshoppers bouncing back and forth among its green stalks, the smell of earth rising up at you everywhere you turned, and as time went on, he understood that if he and Dick had anything in common, it was this deep, irrational love of lawn. It was their bond, but it was also the source of their greatest philosophical differences. For Mr. Bones, the lawn's beauty was a gift from God, and he felt it should be treated as holy ground. Dick believed in that beauty as well, but he knew that it had been born out of human effort, and if that beauty was to last, then unending care and diligence were required. The term was *lawn maintenance*, and until the middle of November not a week went by when Dick did not devote at least one full day to trimming and mowing his quarter-acre patch of sward. He had his own machine – an orange-and-white vehicle that looked like a cross between a golf cart and a midget tractor – and every time he started up the engine, Mr. Bones felt certain that he would die. He hated the noise of that contraption, hated the ear-splitting fury of its spurts and stutters, hated the gasoline smells it deposited in every corner of the air. He would hide in his doghouse whenever Dick roared out into the yard on that thing, burying his head under his blankets in a futile effort to block up his ears, but there was really no escape, no solution short of being let out of the yard altogether. But Dick had his rules, and since Mr. Bones was supposed to be in the yard, the pilot pretended not to notice the dog's suffering. The weeks rolled by, and as the assaults on Mr. Bones's ears continued, he couldn't help building up a certain resentment against Dick for refusing to take him into account.

There was no question that things were better when Dick was gone. That was a fact of life, and he learned to accept it in the same way he had once learned to accept his harsh treatment from Mrs. Gurevitch. She had been downright hostile to him in the beginning, and his first year in Brooklyn had been filled with stinging nose-slaps and grumpy tongue-lashings from the old sourpuss, a buildup of bad blood on both sides. But all that had changed, hadn't it? He had won her over in the end, and who knew if the same thing wouldn't happen with Dick as well? In the meantime, he tried not to think about it too much. He had three people to love now, and after spending his whole life as a one-man dog, that was more than enough. Even Tiger was beginning to show some promise, and once you learned how to stay clear of his pinching little fingers, he could actually be fun to be with – in small doses. With Alice, however, no dose was too large. He wished that she were able to spend more time with him, but she was off at that blasted school all day, and what with the after-school ballet lessons on Tuesday and the piano lessons on Thursday, not to speak of the homework she had to do every evening, their weekday visits were usually confined to a short early-morning conversation – as she straightened his blankets and replenished his food and water bowls – and then, after she returned home, to the period just before dinner, when she would report on what had happened to her since the morning and ask him how his day had gone. That was one of the things he liked best about her: the way she talked to him, calmly moving from point to point without leaving anything out, as if there was never any question that he couldn't understand what she was saying. Alice spent most of her time living in a world of imaginary beings, and she brought Mr. Bones into that world and made him her partner, her fellow protagonist, her male lead. Saturdays and Sundays were full of these screwball improvisations. There was the tea party they attended at the castle of the Baroness de Dunwitty, a beautiful but dangerous Machiavel plotting to take over the kingdom of Floriania. There was the earthquake in Mexico. There was the hurricane on the Rock of Gibraltar, and there was the shipwreck that left them stranded on the shores of Nemo Island, where the only food consisted of twig nubs and acorn shells, but if you managed to find the magic night crawler who lived just under the surface of the ground and ate him up in a single bite, you would be endowed with the ability to fly. (Mr. Bones swallowed the worm she gave him, and then, with Alice clinging to his back, he took off into the air and they escaped the island.)

Tiger was running and jumping. Alice was words and the meeting of minds. She was the old soul in the young body who had talked her parents into letting him stay, but now that he was there and had spent some time among them, he knew that Polly was the one who needed him most. After several dozen mornings of following her around, of listening to what she told him and watching what she did, Mr. Bones understood that she was a prisoner of circumstances just as much as he was. She had been only eighteen when she met Dick. It was just after she graduated from high school, and to earn some money before starting N. C.–Charlotte in the fall, she had taken a summer waitressing job at a seafood restaurant in Alexandria, Virginia. The first time Dick came in, he wound up asking her for a date. He was nine years older than she was, and she found him so handsome and sure of himself that she let herself go farther than she had intended. The romance continued for three or four weeks, and then she went back to North Carolina to start college. She was planning to get a degree in education and become a schoolteacher, but one month into her first term, she discovered that she was pregnant. When she broke the news to her parents, they were outraged. They told her that she was a slut, that she had disgraced them with her promiscuity, and then they refused to offer any help – which caused a rift in the family that was never fully repaired, not even after nine years of apologies and contrition on both sides. It wasn't that she wanted to marry Dick, but after her own father turned his back on her, where else was she going to go? Dick said he loved her. He kept telling her that she was the prettiest, most remarkable girl on the face of the earth, and after a couple of months of wavering back and forth, of sinking into the most desperate kinds of speculation (an abortion, giving up the baby for adoption, keeping the baby and trying to make it on her own), she buckled under the pressure and quit school to marry Dick. Once the baby was old enough, she figured she would be able to go back to college, but Alice was born with all sorts of medical problems, and for the next four years Polly's life was taken up with doctors, hospitals, and experimental surgeries, an endless round of cures and consultations to keep her little girl alive. It was her proudest accomplishment as a human being, she told Mr. Bones one morning – the way she'd looked after Alice and pulled her through – but even though she'd been no more than a young girl herself at the time, she wondered if it hadn't drained her strength for ever. Once Alice was well enough to go to school, Polly began to think about going back to school herself, but then she got pregnant with Tiger, and she had to put it off again. Now it was probably too late. Dick was starting to earn good money, and when you combined his salary with some of the investments he'd made, they were pretty well off now. He didn't want her to work, and whenever she said that maybe it would be nice to work anyway, he always gave her the same answer. She already had a career, he said. Wife and mother was a tough enough job for any woman, and as long as he could take care of her, why change things just for the sake of changing them? And then, to prove how much he loved her, he went out and bought her this big, beautiful house.

Polly loved the house, but she didn't love Dick. This had become manifestly clear to Mr. Bones, and although Polly herself didn't know it yet, it wouldn't be long before the truth finally came crashing down on top of her. That was why she needed Mr. Bones, and because he loved her more than any other living person in the world, he was glad to serve as her confidant and sounding board. There was no one else to fill this role for her, and even though he was a mere dog who could neither counsel her nor answer her questions, his simple presence as an ally was enough to give her the courage to take certain steps she might not have taken otherwise. Establishing her own rules about letting him into the house was hardly a serious matter, but in its own small way it was an act of defiance against Dick, a microscopic instance of betrayal that could, in time, lead to bigger, more significant betrayals. Mr. Bones and Polly both knew that Dick didn't want him in the house, and this injunction only added to the pleasure of his visits, giving them a dangerous, clandestine quality, as if he and Polly were accomplices in a palace revolt against the king. Mr. Bones had been drafted into a war of nerves and smoldering antagonisms, and the longer he was there, the more crucial his role became. Instead of arguing about themselves, Dick and Polly now argued about him, using the dog as an excuse to advance their separate causes, and while Mr. Bones was rarely privy to the conversations, he learned enough from hearing Polly talk to her sister on the phone to know that some fierce battles had been fought on his account. The hair-on-the-carpet skirmish was just one example. Polly always took care to eliminate Mr. Bones's traces from the house when Dick was about to return, assiduously vacuuming every spot where the dog had been, even getting down on her hands and knees when necessary and using strips of scotch tape to remove any vagrant hairs that the machine had missed. Once, however, when Polly had done a less than thorough job, Dick discovered a few strands of Mr. Bones's fur lying on the living-room carpet. As Polly reported the incident to her sister Peg in Durham, those bits of fluff had led to a prolonged and churlish confrontation. "Dick asks me what those hairs are doing there," she said, sitting on a kitchen stool and smoking one of her infrequent morning cigarettes, "and I tell him I don't know, maybe they fell off one of the kids. Then he goes upstairs into the bedroom and finds another one on the floor by the night table. He comes out holding the thing between his fingers and says, I suppose you don't know about this either, and I say no, why should I? Maybe it came from Sparky's brush. His brush? Dick says, what are you doing with his brush in the bedroom? Cleaning it, I say, just as calm as I can be, what difference does it make? But Dick won't let it end there. He's got to get to the bottom of the mystery, and so he keeps on pushing. Why didn't you clean it out in the yard, he says, where you're supposed to? Because it was raining, I say, telling about my fourteenth fib of the conversation. They why didn't you do it in the garage? he asks. Because I didn't want to, I say. It's too dark in there. And so, he says, really starting to get pissed-off now, you drag in the dog's brush and clean it on the bed. That's right, I say, I cleaned it on the bed because that's where I felt like cleaning it, and he says, don't you think that's disgusting, Polly? Don't you know how much I hate that? I'm telling you, Peg, it went on like that for ten more minutes. All this petty bullshit, it drives me crazy sometimes. I can't stand lying to him, but what else am I supposed to do when we start in on these stupid disagreements? He's such a stickler, that man. His heart's in the right place, but half the time he forgets where it is. Jesus. If I told him I was letting the dog into the house, he'd probably divorce me. He'd just pack up his bags and walk out."

Such was the marital turmoil that Mr. Bones had stumbled into. Sooner or later, something was bound to give, but until Polly woke up to herself and finally pushed that piker out the door, the atmosphere would continue to be charged with intrigues and buried animosities, the plots and counterplots of dying love. Mr. Bones did his best to adjust to all this. So much was still new to him, however, so many things still had to be studied and made sense of, that the ups and downs of Polly's marriage occupied no more than a small fraction of his energies. The Joneses had introduced him to a different world from the one he had known with Willy, and not a day went by when he didn't experience some sudden revelation or feel some pang about what had been missing from his former life. It wasn't just the daily rides in the van, and it wasn't just the regular meals or the absence of ticks and fleas from his coat. It was the barbecues on the back patio, the Porterhouse steak bones he was given to gnaw on, the weekend outings to Wanacheebee Pond and the swims with Alice in the cool water, the overall feeling of splendor and well-being that had engulfed him. He had landed in the America of two-car garages, home-improvement loans, and neo-Renaissance shopping malls, and the fact was that he had no objections. Willy had always attacked these things, railing against them in that lopsided, comic way of his, but Willy had been on the outside looking in, and he had refused to give any of it a chance. Now that Mr. Bones was on the inside, he wondered where his old master had gone wrong and why he had worked so hard to spurn the trappings of the good life. It might not have been perfect in this place, but it had a lot to recommend it, and once you got used to the mechanics of the system, it no longer seemed so important that you were tethered to a wire all day. By the time you had been there for two and a half months, you even stopped caring that your name was Sparky.

5

The concept of the family vacation was entirely
unknown to him. Back in Brooklyn as a pup, he
had sometimes heard Mrs. Gurevitch use the
word *vacation*, but never in any way that could be
connected to the word *family*. Suddenly breaking
off from her housework, *Mom-san* would plop
down on the sofa, throw her feet up on the coffee
table, and let out a long, passionate sigh. "That's
it," she would say. "I'm on vacation." According
to this usage, the word seemed to be a synonym
for *sofa*, or perhaps it was simply a more elegant
way to describe the act of sitting down. In either
case, it had nothing to do with families – and
nothing to do with the idea of travel. Travel was
what he did with Willy, and in all the years they
had spent on the road together, he couldn't
remember a single instance in which the word
vacation had crossed his master's lips. It might
have been different if Willy had been gainfully
employed somewhere, but except for a few odd
jobs picked up along the way (sweeping floors in
a Chicago bar, messenger-service trainee for an
outfit in Philadelphia), he had always been his
own boss. Time had flowed without interruption

for them, and with no need to break down the calendar into work periods and rest periods, no particular call to observe national holidays, anniversaries, or religious feast days, they had lived in a world apart, free of the clock-watching and hour-counting that took up so much of everyone's else's time. The only day of the year that had stood out from the others was Christmas, but Christmas wasn't a vacation, it was a work-day. Come December twenty-fifth, no matter how exhausted or hungover Willy might have been, he had always climbed straight into his Santa Claus costume and spent the day walking around the streets, spreading hope and good cheer. It was his way of honoring his spiritual father, he said, of remembering the vows of purity and self-sacrifice he had taken. Mr. Bones had always found his master's talk about peace and brotherhood a bit too sappy for his taste, but painful as it sometimes was to see their dinner money wind up in the hands of a person who was better off than they were, he knew there was a method to Willy's madness. Good begets good; evil begets evil; and even if the good you give is met by evil, you have no choice but to go on giving better than you get. Otherwise – and these were Willy's exact words – why bother to go on living?

Alice was the one who first spoke the words *family vacation* to him. It was the Saturday after Thanksgiving, and she had just come out to the yard with a clear plastic bag filled with turkey leftovers and stuffing – more miracles from Polly's white kitchen. Before Alice emptied the food into his bowl, she squatted down beside him and said, "It's all set, Sparky. We're going on a family vacation. Next month when I'm off from school, Daddy's taking us to Disney World." She sounded so happy and excited about it that Mr. Bones assumed it was good news, and since it never occurred to him that he wasn't included in Alice's *we* and *us*, he found himself more interested in the food he was about to eat than in the possible consequences of this new term. It took him about thirty seconds to polish off the turkey, and then, after lapping up half a bowl of water, he stretched out on the grass and listened to Alice as she filled him in on the details. Tiger was going to love seeing Mickey Mouse and Donald Duck, she said, and even though she'd outgrown those childish things herself, she could remember how much she'd loved them when she was small, too. Mr. Bones knew who this Mickey Mouse character was, and based on the things he'd been told, he wasn't too impressed. Who ever heard of a mouse with a pet dog? It was laughable, really, an insult to good taste and common sense, a perversion of the natural order of things. Any half-wit could have told you that it should be the other way around. Big creatures lorded it over small creatures, and if there was one thing he was certain about in this world, it was that dogs were bigger than mice. How puzzling it was for him, then, as he lay on the grass that Saturday afternoon in late November, to hear Alice talk so enthusiastically about their impending trip. He simply couldn't understand why people would want to travel hundreds of miles just to see a pretend mouse. There might not have been many advantages to living with Willy, but no one could accuse Mr. Bones of not having traveled. He had been everywhere, and in his time he had seen just about everything. It wasn't for him to say, of course, but if the Joneses were looking for an interesting place to visit, all they had to do was ask, and he happily would have led them to any one of a dozen lovely spots.

Nothing more was said about the subject for the remainder of the weekend. On Monday morning, however, when the dog overheard Polly talking to her sister on the phone, he realized how badly he had misunderstood what Alice had told him. It wasn't just a matter of driving down to see the mouse and then turning around and heading home, it was two weeks of discombobulation and movement. It was airplanes and hotels, rental cars and snorkeling equipment, restaurant bookings and family discount rates. Not only was there Florida, there was North Carolina as well, and as Mr. Bones listened to Polly discuss the arrangements for spending Christmas in Durham with Peg, it finally dawned on him that wherever this family vacation was going to take them, he wasn't going along. "We need a break," Polly was saying, "and maybe this will do us some good. Who the hell knows, Peg, but I'm willing to give it a shot. My period's ten days late, and if that means what I think it does, then I have some pretty fast thinking to do." Then, after a short silence: "No. I haven't told him yet. But this trip was his idea, and I'm trying to read that as a good sign." Another silence followed, and then, at last, he heard the words that told him what *family vacation* really meant: "We'll put him in a kennel. There's supposed to be a nice one about ten miles from here. Thanks for reminding me, Peg. I'd better get started on it right away. Those places can get awfully crowded around Christmastime."

He stood there and waited for her to finish, watching her with one of those dreary, stoical looks that dogs have been giving to people for forty thousand years. "Don't worry, Spark Plug," she said, hanging up the phone. "It's only two weeks. By the time you start to miss us, we'll already be back." Then, bending down to give him a hug, she added: "Anyway, I'm going to miss you a lot more than you miss me. You've gotten under my skin, old doggy, and I can't live without you."

All right, they were coming back. He was fairly confident of that now, but that didn't mean he wouldn't have preferred to go with them. Not that he had any great longing to be cooped up in a Florida hotel room or to ride in the baggage compartments of airplanes, but it was the principle of the thing that bothered him. Willy had never left him behind. Not once, not under any circumstances, and he wasn't used to this kind of handling. Perhaps he had been spoiled, but in his book there was more to canine happiness than just feeling wanted. You also had to feel necessary.

It was a setback, but at the same time he knew it wasn't the end of the world. He had learned that now, and all things being equal, Mr. Bones probably would have recovered from his disappointment and served out his prison term with docile good grace. He had been through worse hardships than this one, after all, but three days after receiving the bad news, he felt the first of several painful twinges in his abdomen, and over the next two and a half weeks the pains spread into his haunches, his limbs, and even into his throat. Evil spirits were lurking inside him, and he knew that Burnside was the one who had put them there. The quack had been too busy looking at Polly's legs to examine him properly, and he must have missed something, must have forgotten to run a test or look at his blood under the right microscope. The symptoms were still too vague to produce any outward manifestations (no vomiting, no diarrhea, no seizures as of yet), but as the days wore on, Mr. Bones felt less and less like himself, and instead of taking this family vacation business in his stride, he began to sulk and brood about it, to worry it into a thousand component parts, and what at first had seemed to be no more than a small bump in the road was turned into a full-scale misfortune.

It wasn't that the kennel was such a bad place. Even he could see that, and when Alice and her father deposited him there on the afternoon of December seventeenth, Mr. Bones had to admit that Polly had done her homework. Dog Haven was no Sing Sing or Devil's Island, no internment camp for abused and neglected animals. Situated on a twenty-acre property that had once been part of a large tobacco plantation, it was a four-star rural retreat, a canine hotel designed to accommodate the needs and whims of the most indulged and demanding pets. The sleeping cages lined the east and west walls of a cavernous red barn. There were sixty of them, with ample space provided for each of the boarders (more ample, in fact, than Mr. Bones's doghouse at home), and not only were they cleaned every day, but each one came with a soft, freshly laundered quilt and a chewable rawhide toy – in the shape of a bone, a cat, or a mouse, depending on the owner's preference. Just beyond the back door of the barn, there was an enclosed two-acre meadow that served as an exercise field. Special diets were available, and weekly baths were given at no extra charge.

But none of that mattered, at least not to Mr. Bones. These new surroundings failed to impress him, to arouse even the slightest show of interest, and even after he was introduced to the owner, the owner's wife, and various members of the staff (all of them solid, pleasant pro-doggers), he still had no desire to stay. That didn't prevent Dick and Alice from leaving, of course, and while Mr. Bones wanted to howl out his objections to the rotten thing they'd done to him, he certainly couldn't find fault with Alice's tearful and loving farewell. In his own terse way, even Dick seemed a little sorry about having to say good-bye. Then they climbed into the van and took off, and as Mr. Bones watched them chug down the dirt road and disappear behind the main house, he had his first inkling of the kind of trouble he was in. It wasn't just a case of the blues, he realized, and it wasn't just because he was scared. Something was seriously wrong with him, and whatever mayhem had been brewing in him lately was about to come to a full boil. His head hurt, and his belly was on fire, and a weakness had invaded his knees that suddenly made standing difficult. They gave him food, but the thought of food made him sick. They offered him a bone to chew on, but he turned his head away. Only water was acceptable, but when they pushed the water in front of him, he stopped drinking after two sips.

He was put in a cage between a wheezing ten-year-old bulldog and a luscious golden Lab. Ordinarily, a female of that caliber would have sent him into spasms of lustful sniffing, but that night he barely had the strength to acknowledge her presence before dropping on to his quilt and passing out. Within moments of losing consciousness, he was dreaming about Willy again, but this dream was nothing like the ones that had come before it, and instead of gentle encouragements and soothing rationalities, he was given a full taste of his master's wrath. Perhaps it was the fever burning inside him, or perhaps something had happened to Willy in Timbuktu, but the man who came to Mr. Bones that night was not the Willy he had known in life and death for the past seven and three quarters years. This was a vengeful and sarcastic Willy, a devil Willy, a Willy bereft of all compassion and kindness, and poor Mr. Bones was so terrified of this person that he lost control of his bladder and peed on himself for the first time since he was a pup.

To confuse matters even more, the false Willy was identical in appearance to the true Willy, and when he turned up in the dream that night he was wearing the same tattered Santa Claus gear that the dog had seen him in for the past seven Christmases. Even worse, the dream wasn't set in some familiar place from the past – like the one in the subway car, for instance – but in the present, in the very cage where Mr. Bones was spending the night. He closed his eyes, and when he opened them again in the dream, there was Willy, sitting in the corner just two feet away from him, leaning his back against the bars. "I'm only going to say this once," he began, "so listen up and keep your trap shut. You've turned yourself into a joke, a tired and disgusting joke, and I forbid you to let me into your thoughts anymore. Don't forget that, mutt. Emblazon it upon the doorposts of your palace, and never use my name again – not in vain, not in love, not in any way at all. I'm dead, and I want to be left in peace. All this complaining, all this bitching about what's happened to you – do you think I don't hear it? I'm sick of listening to you, dog, and this is the last time you'll ever see me in your dreams. Do you understand that? Let go of me, birdbrain. Give me some room. I have friends now, and I don't need you anymore. You got it? Butt out of my business and stay out. I'm finished with you."

By morning, the fever had shot up so high that he was seeing double. His stomach had been turned into a battleground of warring microbes, and every time he moved, stirred even an inch or two from where he was lying, another attack would begin. It felt as if depth charges were being detonated inside his bowels, as if poison gases were eating away at his inner organs. He had woken up several times during the night, retching uncontrollably until the pains had been appeased, but none of these lulls had lasted very long, and when day finally broke and light came pouring down through the rafters of the barn, he saw that he was surrounded by half-a-dozen puddles of vomit: little clumps of dried-out mucus, half-digested meat fragments, specks of congealed blood, yellowish broths that had no name.

A great racket was swirling around him by then, but Mr. Bones was too ill to take notice. The other dogs were up and about, barking in anticipation of the day ahead, but the best he could do was lie there in his torpor, contemplating the bollix his body had made of things. He knew that he was sick, but exactly how sick, and exactly where this sickness was taking him, he had no idea. A dog could die from a thing like this, he told himself, but a dog could also recover and be good as new in a couple of days. Given the choice, he would have preferred not to die. In spite of what had happened in the dream last night, he still wanted to live. Willy's unprecedented cruelty had stunned him, had made him feel miserable and unspeakably alone, but that didn't mean that Mr. Bones wasn't ready to forgive his master for what he had done. You didn't turn your back on a person for letting you down just once – not after a lifetime of friendship, you didn't, and especially not if there were extenuating circumstances. Willy was dead, and who knew if dead people didn't grow bitter and nasty after they had been dead for a while? Then again, maybe it hadn't been Willy at all. The man in the dream could have been an impostor, a demon dressed in Willy's form who had been sent from Timbuktu to trick Mr. Bones and turn him against his master. But even if it had been Willy, and even if his remarks had been stated in an excessively hurtful and mean-spirited way, Mr. Bones was honest enough to admit that they contained a germ of truth. He had spent too much time feeling sorry for himself lately, had frittered away too many precious hours pouting over infinitesimal slights and injustices, and that kind of behavior was unseemly in a dog of his stature. There was much to be thankful for, and much life still to be lived. He knew that Willy had told him never to think about him again, but Mr. Bones couldn't help it. He was in that churning, semi-delirious state that high fevers bring, and he could no more control the thoughts that flitted in and out of his head than he could stand up and unlock the door of his cage. If Willy happened to be in his thoughts now, there wasn't much he could do about it. His master would just have to cover his ears and wait until the thought went away. But at least Mr. Bones wasn't complaining anymore. At least he was trying to be good.

Less than a minute after thinking about the

door of his cage, a young woman came and undid the latch. Her name was Beth, and she was wearing a puffy blue nylon parka. Chubby thighs, an inordinately round face, Little Lulu haircut. Mr. Bones remembered her from the day before. She was the one who had tried to feed him and give him water, the one who had patted him on the head and told him he would feel better in the morning. A nice girl, but not much of a diagnostician. The piles of vomit seemed to alarm her, and she crouched down and entered the cage to take a closer look. "Not such a good night, was it, Sparky?" she said. "I think maybe we should show you to Dad." Dad was the man from yesterday, he remembered, the one who had given them the tour of the grounds. A burly guy with black bushy eyebrows and no hair on his head. His name was Pat – Pat Spaulding or Pat Sprowleen, he couldn't recall which. There was a wife in the picture as well, and she had accompanied them on the first part of the walk. Yes, now it was coming back to him, the odd thing about the wife. Her name was Pat, too, and Mr. Bones remembered that Alice had found that funny, had even laughed a little when she heard the two names together, and Dick had pulled her aside and told her to remember her manners. Patrick and Patricia. Pat and Pat for short. It was all so confusing, so terribly inane and confusing.

Eventually, Beth coaxed him to stand up and walk over to the house with her. He threw up once along the way, but the cold air felt good against his hot body, and once the gunk had been expelled from his system, his pains seemed to lighten considerably. Encouraged, he followed her into the house, then gratefully accepted her offer to lie down on the living-room rug. Beth went off to look for her father, and Mr. Bones, already curled up in front of the fireplace, turned his attention to the sounds coming from the grandfather clock in the hall. He heard ten ticks, twenty ticks, and then he closed his eyes. Just before he went under, there was a small disturbance of approaching footsteps, and then a man's voice said, "Leave him be for now. We'll see how he is when he wakes up."

He slept through the morning and deep into the afternoon, and when he woke up he sensed that the worst of it was behind him. It wasn't that he was in top form, but at least he was half alive now, and with his temperature down by a couple of degrees, he could move his muscles without feeling that his body was made of bricks. He was well enough to accept a little water, in any case, and when Beth called her father in to judge the dog's condition for himself, Mr. Bones's thirst got the better of him, and he kept drinking until the water was gone. That was a bad miscalculation. He was in no shape to handle such a prodigious amount, and the instant Pat One entered the room, Mr. Bones promptly barfed the contents of his stomach on to the living-room rug.

"I wish to hell people wouldn't dump their sick dogs on us," the man said. "All we need is for this one to croak. We'll have one pretty lawsuit on our hands then, won't we?"

"Do you want me to call Dr. Burnside?" Beth asked.

"Yeah. Tell him I'm on my way over." He started to leave the room, but halfway to the door he stopped and turned to Beth again. "On second thought, maybe your mother should do it. Things are awfully busy around here today."

That was a lucky break for Mr. Bones. In the time it took for them to track down Pat Two and organize the trip, he was able to work out a plan. And without a plan, he never would have been able to do what he did. It made no difference to him whether he was sick or well, whether he was going to live or going to die. They had presented him with the last straw, and over his dead body would he ever allow them to take him to that moron of a vet. That was why he needed a plan. He would have only a few seconds to pull it off, and the whole thing had to be shining in his head before it happened – so he would know exactly what to do and exactly when to do it.

Pat Two was an older version of Beth. A bit broader in the beam, perhaps, with a red parka instead of a blue one, but she gave off the same air of mannish competence and stolid good humor. Mr. Bones liked both of them better than Pat One, and he felt a little sorry about abusing their trust, especially after they had treated him with such kindness, but this was an all-or-nothing proposition, and there was no time to waste on sentimentality. The woman walked him out to the car on a leash, and just as he knew she would, she opened the passenger door to let him in first, not letting go of the leash until the last possible second. The moment the door slammed shut, Mr. Bones scrambled to the other side of the car and settled into the driver's seat. That was the essence of the strategy, and the trick was to make sure that the leash didn't get tangled up on the gearshift or the steering wheel or any other protrusion (which it didn't) and to be securely in his position by the time she had walked around the front of the car and opened the door on the other side (which he was). That was how he had seen it in his mind, and that was how it happened in the world. Pat Two opened the door on the driver's side, and Mr. Bones jumped out. He hit the ground running, and before she could grab hold of his tail or step on his leash, he was gone.

He headed for the woods on the north side of the main house, trying to keep as far away from the road as possible. He heard Pat Two calling out for him to come back, and a moment later her voice was joined by those of Beth and Pat One. A little after that, he heard the engine of the car turn over and the sound of wheels skidding on dirt, but he was far into the woods by then, and he knew they would never find him. Darkness came early at that time of year, and in another hour they wouldn't be able to see.

He kept going north, trotting along through the frozen underbrush as the dim winter light faded around him. Birds scattered as he approached, soaring up into the high branches of the pines, and squirrels ran off in all directions when they heard him coming. Mr. Bones knew where he was going, and even if he didn't know exactly how to get there, he was counting on his nose to point him in the right direction. The Joneses' backyard was only ten miles away, and he figured he would arrive by tomorrow, the day after that at the latest. Never mind that the Joneses were gone and wouldn't be returning for another two weeks. Never mind that his food was locked up in the garage and he had no way of getting at it. He was only a dog, and he wasn't capable of thinking that far ahead. For now, the only thing that mattered was to get where he was going. Once he did, the rest would take care of itself.

Or so he thought. But the sad truth was that Mr. Bones thought wrong. If he had been at full strength, there's no doubt that he would have reached his destination, but his body wasn't up to the demands he was making on it, and all this jumping and running soon took its toll. Ten miles was not a long journey, not when compared to the monumental treks he had undertaken as recently as three and a half months ago, but he was traveling on an empty tank now, and a dog could go only just so far on pure willpower. Remarkably, he managed to cover almost two miles in that weakened state. He went as far as his legs could carry him, and then, between one step and the next, without the slightest premonition of what was about to happen, he sank to the ground and fell asleep.

For the second time in two nights, he dreamed about Willy, and once again the dream was unlike any of the others that had come before it. This time they were sitting on the beach in La Jolla, California, a place they had visited on their first trip together, before he was fully grown. That meant it was years and years ago, and he was back in the days when everything was new and unfamiliar to him, when everything that happened was happening for the first time. The dream started in the middle of the afternoon. The sun was shining brightly, a small breeze was stirring, and Mr. Bones was lying with his head on Willy's lap, savoring the feel of his master's fingertips as they moved back and forth across his skull. Had any of this really happened? He couldn't remember anymore, but it felt vivid enough to be real, and that was all that concerned him now. Pretty girls in bathing suits, ice-cream wrappers and tubes of suntan lotion, red Frisbees wobbling through the air. That's what he saw when he opened his eyes in the dream, and he could smell the strangeness and the beauty of it, as if a part of him already knew that he was beyond the boundaries of hard fact. It seemed to begin in silence, silence in the sense of no words, with the sound of the waves washing in and out on the shore and the wind flapping the flags and beach umbrellas. Then a pop tune started playing on a radio somewhere, and a woman's voice was singing *be my baby, be my baby, be my baby now*. It was a lovely song, a lovely and stupid song, and Mr. Bones got so caught up in listening to it that he failed to realize that Willy was talking to him. By the time he turned his attention to his master, he had already missed several sentences, perhaps whole paragraphs of vital information, and it took a few moments before he managed to piece together the gist of what Willy was saying.

"Make amends" was the first thing he heard, followed by "sorry, old boy" and "test." When those words were succeeded by "ugly business" and "charade," Mr. Bones was well on his way to catching on. The devil Willy had been a trick, a ruse to tempt him into hardening his heart against his master's memory. Wrenching as the ordeal had been, it was the only way to test the permanence of the dog's affections. The prankster had tried to break his spirit, and even though Mr. Bones had been scared half to death, he hadn't hesitated to forgive Willy when he woke up in the morning, to shrug off his slanders and false accusations and let bygones be bygones. In this way, without even knowing that he was being judged, he had passed the test. The reward was this dream, this visit to a world of languorous, unending summer and the chance to bask in the warmth of the sun on a cold winter's night, and yet pleasurable and well crafted as this dream was, it was no more than a prelude to something far more important.

"What thing is that?" Mr. Bones heard himself say, and suddenly he was aware of his ability to speak again, to form words as clearly and smoothly as any two-leg yapping in his mother tongue.

"That, for one thing," Willy said.

"What *that*?" Mr. Bones said, not understanding at all. "What thing?"

"What you're doing now."

"I'm not doing anything. I'm just lying here with you on the sand."

"You're talking to me, aren't you?"

"It feels like talking. It sounds like talking. But that doesn't mean I'm really doing it."

"And what if I told you that you were?"

"I don't know. I think I'd get up and do a little dance."

"Well, start dancing, Mr. Bones. When the time comes, you don't have to worry."

"What time, Willy? What are you talking about?"

"When the time comes for you to go to Timbuktu."

"You mean dogs are allowed?"

"Not all dogs. Just some. Each case is handled separately."

"And I'm in?"

"You're in."

"Don't kid me, master. If you're joking now, I don't think I could stand it."

"Believe me, pooch, you're in. The decision's been made."

"And when do I get to go?"

"When the time comes. You have to be patient."

"I have to kick the bucket first, don't I?"

"That's the deal. In the meantime, I want you to be a good boy. Go back to Dog Haven and let them take care of you. When the Joneses come to pick you up, remember how lucky you've been. You can't ask for more than Polly and Alice. Those two are as good as it gets, take my word for it. And another thing: don't fret about that name they gave you. You'll always be Mr. Bones to me. But if it ever starts getting you down, just put it in its Latin form, and you'll feel much better. Sparkatus. It has a nice ring to it, doesn't it? Sparkatus the Dog. Behold yon Sparkatus, the noblest tail-wagger in all of Rome."

Yes, it did have a nice ring to it, a very nice ring to it, and when Mr. Bones woke up just after dawn, the sound of it was still rattling around in his head. So much had changed while he had been asleep, so many things had happened to him between the closing and opening of his eyes, that at first he didn't notice the snow that had fallen during the night, nor did he recognize that the tinkling noises caused by the word *Sparkatus* were in fact the ice-coated branches overhead, slowly creaking in the wind. Reluctant to leave the world of the dream, Mr. Bones only gradually became aware of the intense cold around him, and then, once he began to feel the cold, he became aware of an equally intense heat. Something was burning inside him. The cold was outside, and the heat was inside; his body was covered with snow, and inside his body the fever was back, as fierce and paralyzing as it had been the day before. He took a stab at trying to stand up to shake the snow off his fur, but his legs felt like sponges, and he had to abandon the effort. Maybe later, he told himself, maybe later when the sun came out and the air warmed up a little. Meanwhile, he lay there on the ground and studied the snow. No more than an inch had fallen, but even that was enough to make the world feel like a different place. There was something eerie about the whiteness of snow, he found, something both eerie and beautiful, and as he watched two pairs of sparrows and chickadees pecking away at the ground in search of something to eat, he felt a small ache of sympathy flutter inside him. Yes, even for those useless featherbrains. He couldn't help it. The snow seemed to have brought them all together, and for once he was able to look at them not as nuisances but as fellow creatures, members of the secret brotherhood. Watching the birds, he remembered what Willy had told him about going back to Dog Haven. That was good advice, and if his body had been up to the task, he would have followed it. But it wasn't. He was too weak to go that far, and if he couldn't count on his legs to get him there, then he would have to stay where he was. For want of anything else to do, he ate some snow and tried to remember the dream.

By and by, he began to hear the sounds of cars and trucks, the rumble of early-morning traffic. The sun was just coming up then, and as the snow melted off the trees and dropped to the ground in front of him, Mr. Bones wondered if the highway was as close as it seemed to be. Sounds could be tricky sometimes, and more than once the air had fooled him into thinking a far-off thing was closer than it was. He didn't want to waste his energies on futile efforts, but if the road was where he thought it might be, then maybe he had a chance. The traffic was increasing now, and he could detect all manner of vehicles rushing down the wet highway, an unbroken parade of big cars and small cars, trucks and vans, long-distance buses. A person was at the wheel of each one of them, and if just one of those drivers was willing to stop and help him, then perhaps he would be saved. It would mean climbing up the hill in front of him, of course, and then working his way down the other side, but hard as all that was going to be, it had to be done. The road was somewhere, and he had to find it. The only drawback was that it had to be found on the first try. If he took the wrong path, he wouldn't have the strength to go back up the hill and start again.

But the road was there, and when Mr. Bones finally saw it after forty minutes of struggling past the thorns and outcrops and bulging roots that had blocked his way, after losing his footing and slipping down a dirt embankment, after drenching his fur in the muddy residues of the snow, the sick and feverish dog understood that salvation was at hand. The road was immense, and the road was dazzling: a six-lane super-highway with cars and trucks speeding past in both directions. With the moisture from the melted snow still clinging to the black surface of the road, the metal guardrails, and the branches of the trees that lined the east and west shoulders, and with the winter sun blazing in the sky and beating down on these millions of drops of water, the highway presented itself to Mr. Bones as a spectacle of pure radiance, a field of over-powering light. It was exactly what he had been hoping for, and he knew now that the idea that had come to him during those forty minutes of punishing effort up and down the hill was the only correct solution to the problem. Trucks and cars could carry him away from this place, but they could also crush his bones and make him stop breathing for ever. It was all so clear once you took the long view. He didn't have to wait for the time to come; the time was upon him now. All he had to do was step into the road, and he would be in Timbuktu. He would be in the land of words and transparent toasters, in the country of bicycle wheels and burning deserts where dogs talked as equals with men. Willy would disapprove at first, but that was only because he would think that Mr. Bones had gotten there by taking his own life. But Mr. Bones wasn't proposing anything as vulgar as suicide. He was merely going to play a game, the kind of game that any sick and crazy old dog would play. And that's what he was now, wasn't it? A sick and crazy old dog.

It was called dodge-the-car, and it was a venerable, time-honored sport that allowed every old-timer to recapture the glories of his youth. It was fun, it was invigorating, it was a challenge to every dog's athletic skills. Just run across the road and see if you could avoid being hit. The more times you were able to do it, the greater the champion you were. Sooner or later, of course, the odds were bound to catch up with you, and few dogs had ever played dodge-the-car without losing on their last turn. But that was the beauty of this particular game. The moment you lost, you won.

And so it happened, on that resplendent winter morning in Virginia, that Mr. Bones, a.k.a. Sparkatus, sidekick of the late poet Willy G. Christmas, set out to prove that he was a champion among dogs. Stepping off the grass on to the eastbound shoulder of the highway, he waited for a break in the traffic, and then he began to run. Weak as he was, there was still some spring left in his legs, and once he hit his stride, he felt stronger and happier than he had felt in months. He ran toward the noise, toward the light, toward the glare and the roar that were rushing in on him from all directions.

With any luck, he would be with Willy before the day was out.